A lock
of
Mum's
beautiful
hair before
she cut
it short.

Lucky charms
from Mum
and Dad's
wedding
cake.

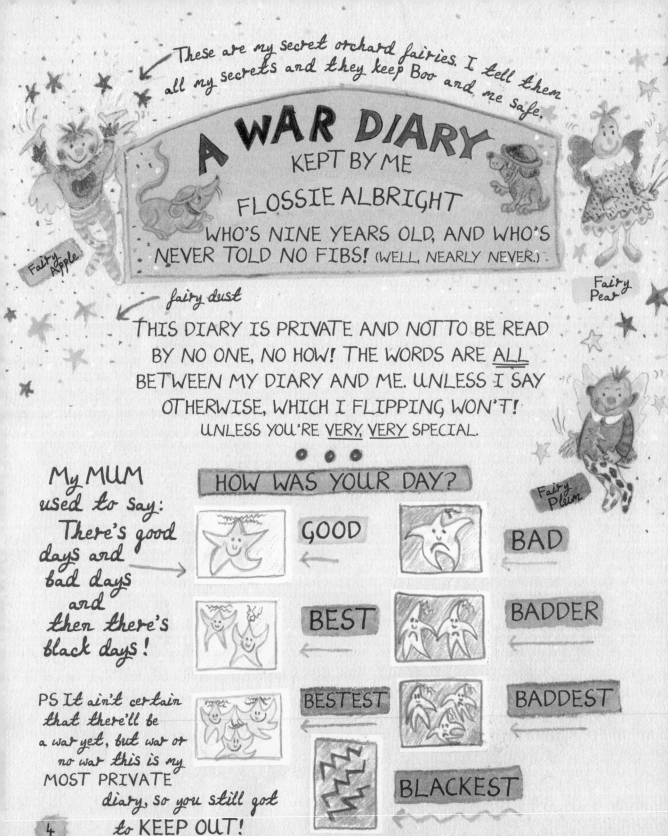

These are my secret orchard fairies. I tell them all my secrets and they keep Boo and me safe.

A WAR DIARY

KEPT BY ME

FLOSSIE ALBRIGHT

WHO'S NINE YEARS OLD, AND WHO'S NEVER TOLD NO FIBS! (WELL, NEARLY NEVER.)

Fairy Apple

Fairy Pear

fairy dust

THIS DIARY IS PRIVATE AND NOT TO BE READ BY NO ONE, NO HOW! THE WORDS ARE <u>ALL</u> BETWEEN MY DIARY AND ME. UNLESS I SAY OTHERWISE, WHICH I FLIPPING WON'T! UNLESS YOU'RE <u>VERY, VERY</u> SPECIAL.

Fairy Plum

My MUM used to say: There's good days and bad days and then there's black days!

PS It ain't certain that there'll be a war yet, but war or no war this is my MOST PRIVATE diary, so you still got to KEEP OUT!

HOW WAS YOUR DAY?

GOOD

BAD

BEST

BADDER

BESTEST

BADDEST

BLACKEST

4

Comic!

My Dad

Great Uncle Colin

Never come between Boo and his bottle!

Boo

Hairgrips - usually getting lost

Summer Me

Freckles!

♥ ♥ ♥

For Recording Events
Most Worthy
of Remembrance

PRIVATE

My freckles turn blue with cold

Winter Me!

More freckles!

knobbly knees!

My Legs

This Diary Belongs To

Flossie Albright
Honeysuckle Cottage
High Barn Estate
Nr Dorchester

FLIPPING

My favourite word

You heard the lass, NO PEEKING !

Food?

Gracie - Great Uncle C's outside dog

Ginger

Milly Mandy

The Outside Cats

Mandy is a boy!

PC Rattle

5

MY DAD GOES
AWAY
AND I GET A DIARY

LEAVE YOUR FAMILY AND JOIN THE FIGHT!

Cheerio!

I LOVE DAD xx

Thursday 27th July 1939

Dear Diary,

I know that you don't know much about me yet – and I will tell – but I just got to write this *first*, 'cos it makes me SO sad...

Miss Joan

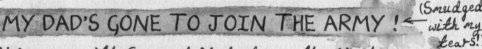

MY DAD'S GONE TO JOIN THE ARMY ! ←

(Smudged with my tears!)

He's gone with General Mole from the big house to join the Dorsetshire Regiment. All men over twenty years have to join the forces now, because we MIGHT go to WAR WITH GERMANY, but I still HATE Dad for going. I do, I flipping DO ... except I don't.

Gen & Mrs Mole

We call the General Old Mouldy, 'cos he's got hair growing out of his ears and it looks like green mould!

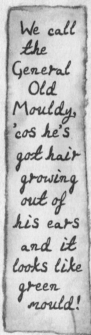

Our Prime Minister, Mr Neville Chamberlain, says there won't be a war, but Miss Joan, the general's daughter, says there will and I believe her. Miss Joan and I were waving our dads off together and she must've noticed that I was welling up. Anyway, when they was gone Cook took Boo and me into the kitchen for some cheering cocoa, and Miss Joan came in and gave me this diary, with a note. (Note on p7.) →

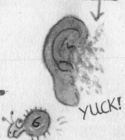

YUCK!

6

Cook

I've never been given stuff from the big house before!

27th July 1939

High Barn Manor
Nr Dorchester
Dorset

Dear Flossie,

I know that you are very upset that your father has joined up, but we must all try to be brave. Mr Adolf Hitler and his Nazi party are determined to take the whole of Europe for themselves, and they will try to exterminate anyone that stands in their way. We must be ready to stop him and to protect those countries and peoples weaker than ourselves, however hard it is to see our fathers go from home.

I hope that this diary will help you get through this difficult time. You can write down all your feelings and tell your own history of the war, if there is one, which I am afraid is almost certain.

Be a brave girl and look after your baby brother, so that your father can be proud of you when he returns home.

Yours sincerely,
Miss Joan

So here I am with no dad, but a posh diary! If anyone sees me with it, I reckon they'll think I nicked it! The paper is a flipping miracle: it's all smooth, with no woody bits. It must've cost a bit!

← My best colour

V. V. IMPORTANT — I DID NOT NICK THIS DIARY ... HONEST!!

Now MY lovely Diary, I've written the sad bit, so if my candle keeps burning, I can tell you about me! I'm nine and a quarter years old and Uncle C says I'm skinny as a whippet. I love to draw, so expect to find your pages covered!

I live with my DAD (well, I did until this afternoon), my Great Uncle Colin, who's too old to fight in a war, and my baby brother, Boo, who's too young — he'll be one next month.

Frizzy red hair — yuck!

Me aged 5 years.

7

A Prayer

Gentle Jesus,
meek & mild,
Look upon
this little
child,
And bring
her dad
back...
QUICK!
Amen.

My dad is Archie Albright and if Mr Hitler kills him, Boo and I will be orphans, 'cos our lovely mum died of the pneumonia after Boo was born. Dad says that if there ain't no war, he'll be back in the shake of a lamb's tail. So I'm going to pray for peace very, very hard and be brave, just like he said.

We live on General Mole's estate in Honeysuckle Cottage. Uncle C is the head gardener – except now that all the under-gardeners have joined up to fight the "maybe war", he's just head of himself. We only got the very young and the very old left on the estate now!

Honeysuckle Cottage

It was during the GREAT WAR that my dad and his brother Ron came to live with Uncle C, on account of the bombs in London... Come to think of it, they were German bombs, so not much has changed.

Uncle Ron got a job on a farm and married Auntie Beth, who runs the village shop. Uncle C taught my dad the country ways.

The Big House

The Orchard

us!

Pond

Granary and stables

Now he's the odd-job man for High Barn Estate. He's ever so clever and can turn his hand to anything!

8

TRAP A HARE   MEND A GATE   FELL A TREE

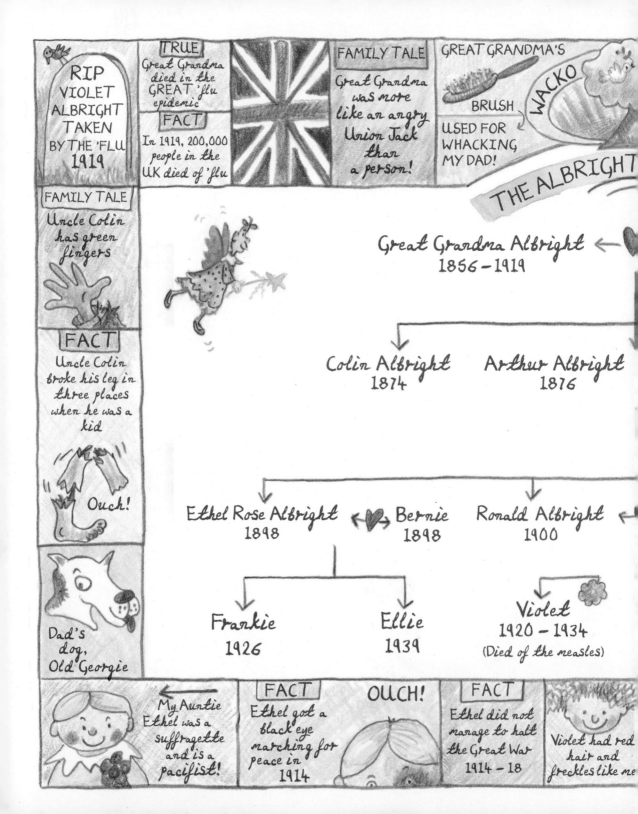

RIP
VIOLET
ALBRIGHT
TAKEN
BY THE 'FLU
1919

TRUE
Great Grandma
died in the
GREAT 'flu
epidemic

FACT
In 1919, 200,000
people in the
UK died of 'flu

FAMILY TALE
Great Grandma
was more
like an angry
Union Jack
than
a person!

GREAT GRANDMA'S
BRUSH
USED FOR
WHACKING
MY DAD!

WACKO

THE ALBRIGHT

FAMILY TALE
Uncle Colin
has green
fingers

FACT
Uncle Colin
broke his leg in
three places
when he was a
kid

Ouch!

Dad's
dog,
Old Georgie

Great Grandma Albright
1856 – 1919

Colin Albright
1874

Arthur Albright
1876

Ethel Rose Albright
1898

Bernie
1898

Ronald Albright
1900

Frankie
1926

Ellie
1939

Violet
1920 – 1934
(Died of the measles)

My Auntie
Ethel was a
suffragette
and is a
pacifist!

FACT
Ethel got a
black eye
marching for
peace in
1914

OUCH!

FACT
Ethel did not
manage to halt
the Great War
1914 – 18

Violet had red
hair and
freckles like me

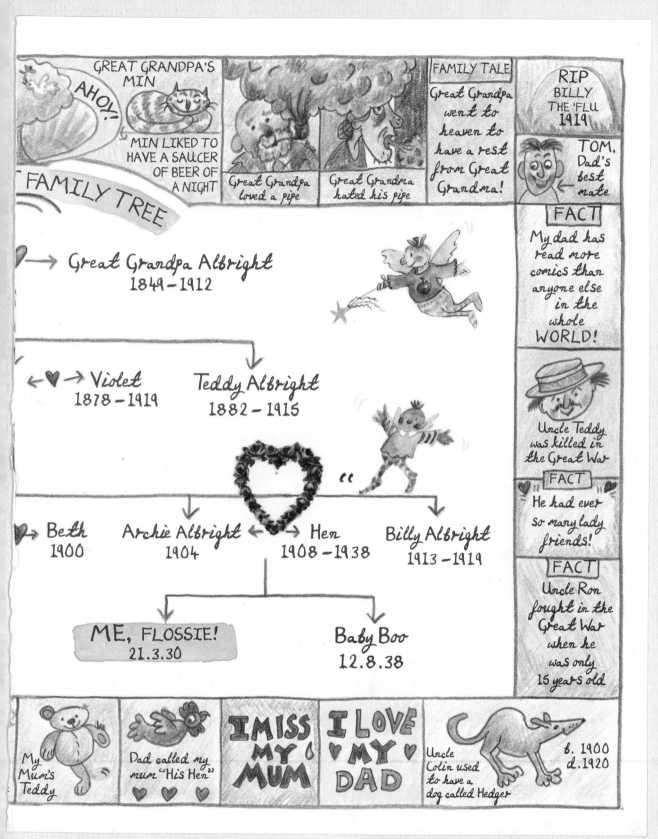

Friday 28th July 1939

LOOKING AFTER BABY BOO AND UNCLE C...

ALL BY MYSELF!!!

Uncle C

Boo

Dear Diary,

I tell you, I ~~ain't~~ haven't had much time to think today, never mind write! Boo and Uncle C take some looking after! Boo is so <u>wild</u>. He isn't walking yet, but when I was trying to change his nappy he pulled himself up by a chair and did a poo on the floor.

Q: Did he laugh? A: Yes!
Q: Did I laugh? A: No!

The good bit was that even though I was up writing half the night, I still got up in time to give Uncle C his lunch, all wrapped up nice.

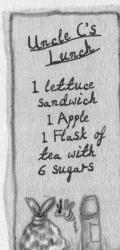

Uncle C's Lunch

1 lettuce sandwich
1 Apple
1 Flask of tea with 6 sugars

Poo!

He gave me such a big hug, it's kept me going all day ... so poo to you Boo!

Boo's having a nap now, so I've escaped to the granary to write. I still can't believe this diary's MINE!!!!

Bonkers, talking to a diary!

Dear Diary, I'm ever so happy to have you, 'cos it isn't going to be easy without my mum or my dad. War or no war, I'll be glad to have you to chat to...AND SHARE MY SECRETS WITH!!

Ooops, Uncle C's lovely dog, Gracie, is nipping my ear and that means Boo's awake!!

10

Saturday 29th July

It was sunny today, so Boo and I helped Uncle C in the garden. Boo ate a worm – I have to watch him every flipping minute! Uncle C says worms are full of protein, so he won't die.

Worms eat apples, so they've got to be good for you!

Flippin' babies!

Sun 30th July 1939

HITLER: BAD

COOK: GOOD

As a treat, Mrs Mole let Bathgate, her ancient groom who looks after the horses, take Boo and me to church in the trap. Boo loved the ride, but without Dad nothing seems much of a treat to me. The vicar says he's sure there'll be a war, on account of Mr Hitler and his Nazi party, but we mustn't think all Germans are bad. Cook gave us our dinner in her kitchen, up at the big house. Cook's right nice to Boo and me – we had Yorkshire puds with gravy!

Tues 8th August WAAAAH!

Boo woke me up THREE TIMES last night! Uncle C says he'll get up for him when I'm back at school, but I bet he won't. For one thing, he's as deaf as a flippin' gatepost, and for another he sleeps downstairs in the kitchen and we're upstairs.

Boo sleeps in a drawer by the bed; he's too big for it really, but if I takes him into bed I wake up stinking of wee ... little blighter!

Dear diary, I will now tell you a secret –

(IT'S ON THE NEXT PAGE!)

snore – snuffle...

11

Boo is just my brother's nickname. When Mum died, Dad didn't seem to have the heart to name him, so I called him Boo. He's nearly a year old now, so I think Dad should give him a proper name — and add a bit to the drawer, so he ain't so squashed.

Weds 9th August 1939

Cook's just told me that Dad's weekend leave has been cancelled. Mrs Mole had a letter from the general. Cook said, "It don't look good for peace, if they're cancelling leave." I wish Dad would write. This is what a postcard looks like, Dad. It don't take long to write and you could make one if you ain't got no money!

I ♥ U!

Thursday 10th

It's so flipping hot – we all feel wilted!

No, no, please don't kill me.

Our water tastes sour, which is a sure sign the well is low. Uncle C says that if it don't rain soon, we'll have to stop watering the flowers and just dribble the veg. I'd hate to see the sweet peas die, 'cos they were Mum's favourite.

THIS WAS FUN!

This picture is for you, Mum: it's me washing Boo in the stream today – he loved it! I try to be good to him for you; I hope you get to see us when we laugh.

We both loves you, Mum.

Friday 11th August '39

Today, me, Boo and Uncle C went to help Uncle Ron with the harvest. Farm workers don't have to join the forces as they're needed to feed us, so Uncle Ron has become our local Air Raid Warden.

12

He has to sound the alarm if the Germans are about to bomb us. He kept putting on his ARW helmet and shouting "Bomb alert!" We laughed and laughed, till Auntie Beth clocked him one and said, "We won't be laughing if they really do bomb us!"

Then Uncle Ron got all serious and told us to prepare for a blackout practice on Monday at 11.20 pm. If he sees even the tiniest chink of light from our cottage, he'll report us and we'll have to pay a fine. That's if the Germans don't spot the light first and bomb us!

"Bomb alert, bomb alert, make for the ditches!"

Sat 12th August 1939

BOO'S 1st BIRTHDAY

Uncle C spent all day making blackout frames. Luckily the cottage is only one up and one down, so there ain't many windows.

Later, Uncle Ron and Auntie Beth came over and Cook popped in with a birthday cake for Boo. He blew the candle out all by himself – I was ever so proud!

Then came the bad bit: Auntie Beth ruined everything by saying I wasn't looking after Boo properly. She said Boo should live with her.

My heart sank, but luckily Uncle C weren't having it. He said Dad had left Boo with us and that was that! Phew! I miss Dad!

Wooden frame card painted black

GOOD

Auntie Beth

Do put a nappy on that baby, Flossie.

Leave the kiddie alone; there's no water for washing nappies and there ain't nothing wrong with a bare bum.

BAD ← Cook

VERY PRIVATE

I don't like Auntie Beth no more. She spoilt Boo's day. "Draw a line under it and start again." That's what Mum used to say, so I'm drawing one under Auntie Beth's horridness, just like Mum said.

Sunday 13th August 1939

No lift to church today! I had to carry that podgy, wriggly Boo all the way, which ain't easy. Uncle C never comes with us because he thinks "priests are meddlesome creatures that should stay down their burrows"! We was late and had to creep in at the back. Boo made faces at the old ladies, I prayed for Dad and peace and the vicar talked about war, war, war. I got so hot carrying Boo home, I nearly gave up and dumped him in the stream.

THEN I got home to find that Uncle C had made Boo a cart. Now I don't have to carry him ~~no more~~ any more! Isn't that GRAND!
I pushed him up to the top of Merry Hill and we watched the big war ships gathering in Weymouth Harbour.

A picture of the vicar peeping out of his burrow! ↓

War, war, war... carrots!

Then I ran all the way down, with Boo squealing and clapping. You should have seen him BUMP!

BUMP!

It works drawing a line under things - thanks, Mum. X

I love Great Uncle C.

14

Nobody told the stars not to shine on blackout night.

Not the Moon!

Tues 15th August 1939

Uncle Ron told us that the pilots who flew over Dorset checking for lights saw chinks all over the place, but not at Honeysuckle Cottage!

BLACK-OUT PRACTICE

Our blackout was perfect. In Weymouth two cyclists were knocked off their bikes, on account of it being so dark. Uncle Ron hadn't given them one of his posters!

LOOK OUT IN THE BLACK-OUT

REGULATION WHITE PATCH ON MUDGUARD

GOOD TYRES AND BRAKES

I wish I could have a bicycle. Then I could bike to school, give Boo a ride to church and go see Dad at The Keep in Dorchester where he's billeted.

Wednesday 16th

A badge for Auntie Ethel!

MAKE PEACE NOT WAR

Today I had a letter from Auntie Ethel in London. Poor thing, she's always marching for peace and will be ever so upset if there's a war.

OPERATION PIED PIPER
The government is planning to evacuate over 3 million children from our cities!

Ain't that something!

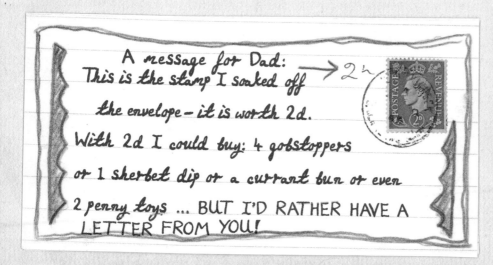

A message for Dad:
This is the stamp I soaked off the envelope – it is worth 2d.

2d

POSTAGE 2d REVENUE

With 2d I could buy: 4 gobstoppers or 1 sherbet dip or a currant bun or even 2 penny toys ... BUT I'D RATHER HAVE A LETTER FROM YOU!

Monday 28th August 1939

We should go back to school this week, but we're NOT! So many men have joined up that us children are needed to bring in the harvest. Not that I can be much help on account of looking after Boo and Uncle C. Boo and I made biscuits today – he made his with his feet!

Kids say "No" to heavy loads!

Tuesday 29th

GAS MASK NIGHTMARE

Dear Diary, Even though there are no classes, we had to go to school today. We were fitted with gas masks in case of a poisonous gas attack. It is such a scary thought – my stomach is all churned up.

The masks stink of rubber and make your face all sweaty. As for breathing in them, forget it! I tried not to make a fuss when mine was fitted, but lots of kids cried and Miss Joan's old nanny fainted. She was given some brandy, so after that lots of oldies fainted ... including Uncle C!

We were given an identity card and a cardboard box with a string handle, 'cos we got to carry our gas masks everywhere we go.

KEEP SMILING – IT MIGHT NEVER HAPPEN!

Our local bobby helped to fit the gas masks. He said:

Hitler will send no warning – so always carry your gas mask.

What does he mean? I didn't think we were at war yet.

MY GAS MASK

THE BOX

MY IDENTITY CARD

FOR OFFICIAL USE ONLY

TOTALLY SECRET!!

Dear Diary, I'm right upset – Boo's too little for a proper gas mask, so he's got a sort of suit thing that I have to pump air into. I think I might kill him if I don't do it right. Uncle C says not to worry – he'll do it – but what if he's not there?

Boo hates the flipping thing and screams at the sight of it.

window
straps
pump
Boo wriggling and screaming inside

I won't be napping for long!

I thought of letting Auntie Beth take him after all, but she don't love him like I do. I miss my mum and dad so much.

No tears, Flossie.

BOO's UP

<u>LATER</u> – Boo's napping and I'm in the granary having a cry. A tiny field mouse is peeping at me. I think he's trying to cheer me up. I've named him Granary Mouse. His whiskers are twitching and he's blinking his little pop-eyes!

He doesn't even seem scared of Gracie, who's come to tell me that Boo's awake. I'll fetch him some cheese later.

LATER STILL

I left the cheese by a grain bin, 'cos I couldn't find my little mouse friend.

When Flossie was little, she'd hide in a grain bin if she'd been naughty.

We had to pull her out!

PC Rattle saved this card for me.

THE CIVILIAN RESPIRATOR –
HOW TO REMOVE IT

Thurs 31st August 1939

There's a right flap on!
A trainload of evacuee
children are arriving from London tomorrow
morning. Cook's been told to expect some because the
house is so big. She's in a real tizz.

DOES MR CHAMBERLAIN THINK THE GERMANS ARE
ABOUT TO BOMB LONDON? ARE WE AT WAR??

The children will 'ave some food and be checked by
a nurse. Then Bathgate will drop some of 'em off at
their billets (that's what their new homes are
called) and bring some of 'em back to the big house.

Afternoon

Institute
cottage as
but she said we hadn't even enough room for a skinny
evacuee. I'd cleaned up special, 'cos I'd like another kid
around. I bet if Mum were here we'd have got one.

A lady from the Women's
has just been to look at our
London is sending extra kiddies,

Baa!

A war? Of course not!

Mr Chamberlain
Our Prime Minister

MOO!

No dear, it wouldn't be hygienic!

WI Woman

Oh my! Oh my! Oh my! Oh my!

This is Cook, flapping!

EVACUEES & MUM

I brought a few mates for you, Floss.

Hurrah!

ME

EXTRA, EXTRA EXCITING NEWS BY THE SECOND POST!!!!!!!!!

ME
(AGAIN)
BEING
EXTRA
HAPPY!

Wacko, my lovely.
The general has
organized a spot
of leave for the
weekend after
this – see you
then. xxxxx Dad

Ripping news!

Flossie Albright
Honeysuckle Cottage
High Barn Estate
Dorchester

Get ready folks, they're here!

EVACUEES!

Dorset special

Sat 2nd September

Dear Diary, Flipping heck ... you should've seen 'em!
I couldn't tell you about it yesterday because our vacs
(that's short for evacuees) didn't arrive until early
evening. Bathgate drew up in the trap with:

Mrs Rose & Baby

'Ere, you take 'im.
Mrs Jones & Baby

I want my mammy!
Maggie & Molly

Simon

Cook wasn't expecting Simon. He's Jewish and has
travelled all the way from Germany, poor mite. There
weren't no room for him anywhere else, so Bathgate
brought him here. I think he's about my age. He's a
sort of grey colour, and has bright, teary eyes.
Not that he cries, eats, or speaks – even in German.
I wonders if he understands English? Cook says he's
come to Britain 'cos them Nazis don't like the Jews.

Oh yes ... you will!

IF YOU OPEN THIS I'LL SET
THEM ORCHARD FAIRIES ON YOU.
THEN YOU'LL BE SORRY!

When the vacs arrived, they had name and address labels
tied to them – they looked like bits of flipping luggage!

A BIT PONGY!

I DON'T MEAN TO BE UNKIND, BUT IT'S TRUE

MAGGIE

- hair - greasy
- sweater - thin and holey
- teddy - one eye, one arm, no legs
- gas mask
- ragged dress

name label
possessions (empty)
no shoes

Pooh!

Q: WHAT DID COOK SAY WHEN SHE SAW THEM?

A: OH MY, OH MY, OH MY!

Maggie and Molly were crying 'cos their poor mum don't even know where they are. Mrs Mole has to send her the special card they brought with them. Cook asked Boo and me in to tea to break the ice, and Mrs Mole and Miss Joan put their heads around the kitchen door and gave the vacs a smile. They should've stayed for tea. We had a feast.
 Uncle C must've got wind of it, because he sneaked in too!

bread   ham   cheese   pickle   jam sponge

radishes   hot milk   or   tea   +   as much sugar as you wanted!!!   farm butter

SIMON DID NOT TOUCH A CRUMB.

<u>Maggie</u> said the milk was too thick - they must water it down in London.
<u>Molly</u> snivelled because the bread was "dirty", not white sliced like in London.
<u>Mrs Rose</u> wanted more of everything.
<u>Mrs Jones</u> put six spoons of sugar in each of her four cups of tea!
· <u>Simon</u> didn't say a word.
<u>Cook</u> said "oh my" a lot and that the evacuee allowance of 8/6 a week wouldn't even keep Mrs J in sugar!

AFTER TEA CAME BATH TIME - NOT POPULAR !!!!!

Meanwhile, while nobody was looking...!

Sorry pet, but it has to be done.

Mouse tea

Straight after tea Uncle C filled the tin bath and in went Maggie and Molly. How they howled! I don't think they'd seen a bath before - no wonder they ponged. London must be ever such a dirty place. They had rags in their hair for ribbons, no knickers and the pair of shoes they had between them had no soles. Their dresses were in tatters and crawling with fleas, so Uncle C had to burn them.

Fleas!

Cook didn't half scrub the poor mites. Then she soaked a couple of towels in paraffin and wrapped up their heads on account of the lice - they ponged even worse then! Once they were swaddled in a blanket Cook started on Simon.

She made a screen around him, so I couldn't see much and he didn't make a squeak. Anyway, after they were spruce, she gave them each one of Miss Joan's old vests and sent them off to sleep in the maids' room, 'cos they're both off working in an army canteen. I think the nuns got the treatment next, but I went home with Boo and Uncle C. I swear we ain't caught fleas, but we don't half itch!

Don't fret, lad!

More fleas!

← Still more fleas! →

21

Sunday 3rd September

Boo and I got up ever so early to go and help Cook with the vacs. (Boo was so excited he took six steps!) Cook was in a right tizzy and the two mums were just sitting on the doorstep drinking tea and moaning. Molly, Maggie and Simon all stank of wee, so one of 'em must've wet the bed, and to top it off, Mrs Mole told Cook they all had to go to church!

Country Life (according to the vacs)

It stinks here!

It's too bloomin' quiet!

A Wild Beast

Oh my, Oh my ...

I only got two hands!

They ain't got a stitch between 'em ...

Not even a pair of shoes! Oh my!

A Walking Cloud

Eventually we got them all fed and dressed in some of Miss Joan's old clothes ('cept Simon of course, 'cos he brought a set of best), and set off across the fields to church.

A Large Sparrow

 WILD BEASTS!

Quackers!

A Bomber!

Help, I've been attacked!

I don't think the vacs had seen farm animals before and when Mrs Jones stepped in a cowpat, you'd have thought it was a flipping land mine! Anyway, it made everyone laugh, 'cept Simon. He's so quiet. I reckon he's missing his mum and dad, just like me. We made it to church just in time.

6pm THAT SAME WAR-DECLARING DAY

WOULD YOU BELIEVE IT!

We was all invited into the hall, up at the big house, to listen to King George VI himself talk on the wireless! King George VI is almost as handsome as my dad!

THE KING'S MESSAGE TO THE EMPIRE

"In this grave hour, perhaps the most fateful in our history, I send to every household of my people, both at home and overseas, this message – for the sake of all that we ourselves hold dear and of the world's order and peace, it is unthinkable that we should refuse to meet the challenge...

I now call my people at home and my people across the seas... to stand firm and united in this hour of trial."

I have to report that we was all moved, so we stood tall for the National Anthem and Dad and General Mole saluted. Then Mrs Mole said we could have tea in the kitchen!

THIS REPORTER CRIES AND BABY BOO GETS A NAME

I didn't go in to tea with the others, 'cos Dad wanted a chat. He told me he had to go back to Dorchester and I cried and there's the truth of it. I could tell you different, but reporters never lie – they has to tell you the good and the bad.

I do not look pretty when I CRY!

Dad said he would try and write more, but better than that, he gave Boo A NAME! It's Tom, after Dad's best friend in London, but we can call him Tommy!

I went in to Cook then, I was too choked to wave Dad off. Cook gave ~~Boo~~ Tommy a saucer of tea and Simon gave me his biscuit! Maybe Simon does understand things, but just don't want to talk... unlike the London rabble – as Cook calls them. They never stop whinging.

EVEN LATER ON THIS FATEFUL SUNDAY

When we got home Uncle C gave us one of his humbugs. I crushed Tommy's, so he wouldn't choke.

Now Uncle C is snoring in bed and Tommy's asleep in his carriage. Uncle C has his humbugs under his pillow, just in case Mr Hitler decides to nick 'em – flipping nuts he is!

I'm writing this at the kitchen table, 'cos we're all staying downstairs tonight – the first night of war.
I got to sleep now – I'm knackered. I'll do some pictures later... so goodnight from Flossie's news desk. If we don't get bombed, I'll be back with more news tomorrow.
Meanwhile, let me leave you with this little teaser:
Q: Which would be worse, a German bomb or a German in uniform?

You are my prisoner!

A: I don't know and I don't ever want to find out.

PREMIER'S HISTORIC DECLARATION

WESTMINSTER, Sunday.
"This country is now at war with Germany."
The sentence came from the Prime Minister's lips in tones of sharp precision.
A profound silence fell upon the House, not of surprise or anxiety but the calm, stern faces testified, but of grim satisfaction.
Hundreds of men on the crowded green benches drew a long breath of relief that the issue was declared and joined beyond a peradventure.
Conditions, circumstance and chance united to invest the Prime Minister's declaration with arresting dramatic force.

As dusk gathered the night before he had made a provisional, ad interim statement which, the words are not too strong, bewildered and shocked the House by its vagueness.
He told members then that he was waiting for the result of consultations with France, but his promise to be definite to-day did not allay the anxieties in which they went home.
Definite he was this Sunday morning. The tragic irony that a proclamation of war which will convulse the world and determine its destinies should be made in the sunshine of a Sunday struck home to every heart.
It happened that the first al war had thrilled through even before he spoke.

Monday 4th Sept   WE AIN'T BEEN BOMBED YET!

Cook let me and Tommy listen to the BBC news in her kitchen. France, Australia and New Zealand have all declared war on Germany so them's our allies. A British ship, the Athenia, was sunk by a German sub in the Atlantic. Loads of passengers died and some were American, but President Roosevelt don't want to join the war. British ships are to travel in convoys now, with war ships to protect them.

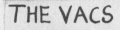

One poo a week is quite enough, Flossie

Sunday 10th September 1939

Dear Diary, We been at war for one week and it don't seem much different, except we got a bucket of earth by the cottage door in case an incendiary bomb sets light to the thatch. It's like the bucket of earth in the outside toilet used to cover our own bombs!

Uncle C hates clearing out the toilet!

Also, we has to practise running for the wine cellar in the big house, in case of an air attack. You should hear Uncle C and Bathgate wheeze and moan!

Attack! Attack!

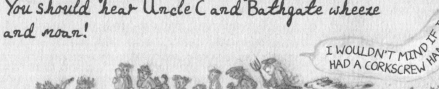

I WOULDN'T MIND IF I HAD A CORKSCREW HANDY!

THE VACS

Well, Jerry ain't dropped no bombs yet!

Mrs Jones detests the country and wants to go back to London! She don't like our food, 'cos it isn't out of tins and she don't like the quiet. She and Mrs Rose walk up the lane to listen for the sound of motors! As petrol is rationed now all they're likely to hear is the odd cow or sheep.

Sooner they go back to London the better!

They don't ever help Cook – she gets spitting mad! Maggie and Molly just sit about scuffing the ground, while Simon is that quiet, he's like a flipping ghost. I wish he'd say something, even if it's in German, 'cos we know he's not our enemy. Cook has to wash their sheets every day, 'cos one of them wets the bed. So does Tommy, but that's 'cos Uncle C and me aren't that good at fixing nappies!

24

WAR IS DECLARED

READ ALL ABOUT IT IN FLOSSIE ALBRIGHT'S NEWS EXTRA

Sunday 3rd September 1939   ONE PENNY!

...l residents ... evacuees were ... gathered for ...day worship, ... our Ron runs ...he vicar looked ...so shocked, ...his voice ...ined steady as ...elayed Ron's message "At 11.15 today, ...e Minister Neville Chamberlain ...unced to the nation that the ...ans have invaded Poland. As they ...ignored all requests to withdraw, ...e now at war with Germany!"

After a prayer for our armed forces the vicar sent everyone home, for fear of a sudden German invasion. In the scramble many personal items were left behind and this reporter forgot to put her posy on her Mum's grave.

WAR IS SCARY!

Outside the sun still shone, but we was scared. I wished my Uncle C were there to put Boo in his gas suit if we was bombed. We scurried across the fields, searching the sky for German bombers. When a sparrow hawk dived for prey near me, I was so scared I nearly tipped Boo out of his cart and that evacuee boy, Simon, cried. I wonders if he can understand what's going on, poor like. Our Gracie licked his face and she stayed close by him from then on, bless her.

FLOSSIE'S DAD RETURNS

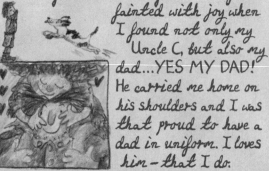

When I got back to the cottage, Uncle C weren't there, so I dragged poor Boo straight to The King's Arms. I fair fainted with joy when I found not only my Uncle C, but also my dad...YES MY DAD! He carried me home on his shoulders and I was that proud to have a dad in uniform. I loves him – that I do.

LATER THE SAME DAY –

A fairy never tells!

Blanket   Feed bin

A STRANGE MYSTERY!

After church a WI woman brought the vacs some blankets, in case of a sudden cold snap. <u>Later</u>, when I went to visit Granary Mouse, I found a blanket hidden behind a feed bin! I ain't said nothin', but I'm keeping a lookout.

As we're so short handed, I showed Tommy how to feed the chickens and ducks today, but he just followed the ducks into the pond with a muddy SPLASH! It's a start, but Uncle C says he thinks he'd best apply for a couple of them land girls to help on the estate!

Some girls is leaving school early to join the land girls. I ain't!

A CAREER FOR WOMEN

WOMENS LAND ARMY

<u>Monday 11th September</u>

BACK TO SCHOOL!!

I took the vacs and Tommy too, 'cos there's nobody to look after him at home. Mr Hardyke, our head, has joined the RAF so now we've got Miss Duncan. She's ever so nice, and she says Tommy can stay as long as he's good. Trouble is, the little tyke don't do "good".

Today, he weed on the floor, tipped up his sand tray and blew bubbles in his milk bottle. I blushed silly, but Miss Duncan just said, "Let him settle." I have to watch him the whole flipping time, but I did have a quick skip with my mates.

TOMMY'S 1st DAY OF SCHOOL

This is our new skipping rhyme:
Heil Hitler, yah, yah, yah!
What a funny little man you are.
With your black moustache and your
Hair all blah! Heil Hitler, yah, yah, yah!

I cut this picture of Hitler out of Cook's paper. He's "blah" all right!

After lunch I helped Maggie write a letter home, because she's not that good at her letters. I made her write one for my diary as well!

School was so full of vacs today, half of us had to sit on the floor!

To der mamy, me and Moly mises yo and aunty cook threw us ribbons away. she says she'll buy us pinc ones frm the gipsys. we aint hd fish and chps and we as to go to skl. Love Magy and Moly. PLS come soon. we got shoes.

Poor Molly and Tommy fell asleep going home — school's good for sleeping! Simon helped me push them in the cart.

Tues 12th Sept   THE MATHS GENIUS

Miss Duncan's new plan: the local kiddies will have morning school and the vacs afternoon school, so it's not such a squash. Only she's left Simon to tag along with me. I reckon it's because he's so clever. When we did our sums he even got the long division right! (He let me copy!)
Miss D says he uses decimal points, but she showed him how to do it our way.

This is the hardest sum we did today!

$$39\overline{)13,756}$$

352
117
2056
195
106
78
28

Leave room for the skippers when you digs up the playground.

In the afternoon we went for a nature ramble with Colonel Stride. He's too old to fight so he's going to look after the group not in school. He says we will learn to march, salute and grow our own food in case of shortages!

WINGS FOR VICTORY!

Feathered wings FOR VICTORY!

I wonder if Dad could see the same plane at the same time as me?

The colonel took us up Barrow Hill to salute the warships in Portland and Weymouth harbours. There are great silver barrage balloons tethered out at sea to stop the German planes coming down low and bombing us. The colonel says not to be scared if we see a German plane flying over because they'll not bomb us, just cities like London, Coventry and Bristol. There are loads of our planes flying about from Warmwell aerodrome, near Dorchester, where they're training new fighter pilots. Sometimes they fly so low you can wave to the crew!

The colonel carried Tommy for me.

Don't worry – I'll save you!

Weds 13th September 1939

A letter from Auntie Ethel and Frankie. He don't half make me laugh!

Frankie, aged 6

Here's a photo of Frankie for your diary like you asked. I ain't got one of me and Ellie, so I done this masterpiece!

MAKE PEACE NOT WAR

Who'd have cousins!

What ho, put the kettle on, Floss!

Pink Salad   Baked Pot   Blackberry Pie

The only magic in these parts is fairy magic!

And mouse magic!

Saturday 16th Sept 1939   Oh happiness!

Dad borrowed a bike and came over for tea!! He said I was magic in the kitchen, just like his Hen (that's my mum). He had to go back straight after, and I was worried on account of the blackout 'cos it's a fair ride to Dorchester. Only Dad said he'd be fine – the bike mudguards were painted white and he had a torch covered in paper to fix to the handlebars.

Anyway, Diary, I cried when he left and there's the truth of it. Cook fetched me over to the big house to listen to the late news – it wasn't cheering!

I'm going to leave a note in the orchard for the fairies, asking 'em to keep my dad safe.

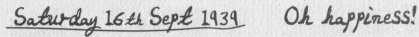

HERE IS FLOSSIE ALBRIGHT WITH THE LATE NEWS EXTRA The British Army has secretly shipped men and arms across the Channel to France! Viscount Gort is their Commander-in-Chief.

I HOPE DAD DOESN'T HAVE TO GO TO FRANCE!

Monday 18th Sept

I ain't slept much on account of worrying about Dad going to France. And now Cook's read me some really bad news from her paper:

Yesterday, H. M. Aircraft Carrier Courageous was struck by a torpedo from a German submarine. 518 of the crew died. The commander, Captain Mackeig-Jones, remained on the bridge and went down with his ship.

Captain Mackeig-Jones

← This is the captain – I cut his picture out of the paper. He looks so kind – I feel for his family. Flippin' war!

I got an answer from the fairies, ain't that something!

Tues 3rd October 1939
IT'S FLIPPING HORRIBLE!

Dad's gone to France with Old Mouldy. It's stupid, 'cos there ain't no fighting in France and I needs him here. What if Tommy gets sick or the flipping Germans invade us? He didn't even say goodbye.

I WON'T HAVE HIM FOR MY DAD NO MORE and I'm chucking Tommy's stupid gasbag and getting him a mask.

I don't know if this is mud or fairy dust.

Dearest Flossie. We're going to keep a special eye on your dad. We already filled his pockets with fairy dust, so don't you go worrying. From your Fairy Friends. xxxxxx

BONJOUR!

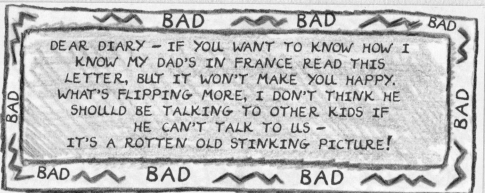

BAD BAD BAD BAD BAD BAD BAD BAD

DEAR DIARY – IF YOU WANT TO KNOW HOW I KNOW MY DAD'S IN FRANCE READ THIS LETTER, BUT IT WON'T MAKE YOU HAPPY. WHAT'S FLIPPING MORE, I DON'T THINK HE SHOULD BE TALKING TO OTHER KIDS IF HE CAN'T TALK TO US – IT'S A ROTTEN OLD STINKING PICTURE!

Sunday 15th October 1939
FLIPPING VICAR SHOULD STICK TO SERMONS!

I've been that down on account of Dad, I ain't felt like writing. I'm only writing today because of what the vicar told us:

Yesterday, the British battleship H.M.S. Royal Oak was torpedoed. 833 seamen lost their lives.

I hates the Jerry. Maybe Dad should fight 'em, but I still don't like him for it.

Tues 31st Oct 1939   I'VE BEEN STUPID!

Dear Diary, I been in the dumps and neglecting you, but Miss Duncan made me cry today and I feels better for it. She said how brave my Dad was going off to war, and how lucky I am to know where he is, unlike Simon, who still ain't heard a word from his family. He don't even know if they're still in Germany.

I'M SORRY!

I wonder if Dad will recognize Mum's old sweater? Them's pretty colours.

Special patterns have been issued for the forces.

Tommy's knitting!

IT'S
A
GOOD
LIFE
IN
THE
LAND ARMY!

NEW WOOLIES FOR OUR SOLDIERS

Wednesday 1st November 1939

Cook's teaching me to knit. We unravelled an old sweater of Mum's and I'm knitting socks and a balaclava for Dad!

Friday 3rd November

Still knitting – even under my desk at school! I've got Uncle C and Tommy at it too! I told Tommy his was a bit small for Dad, but perfect for my diary... he was ever so proud!

Saturday 11th Nov   LAND GIRLS AHOY!

There's another flap on! Two land girls is arriving by train this afternoon to fill in for our workers who joined up. Bathgate has already gone to fetch them. Cook is fit to burst.

Lilly

Them's pretty

Nessy

Cook has the "oh my's"!

Oh my, oh my, where's them to sleep? Oh my, oh my, I 'ope her upstairs ain't expecting me to feed land girls as well as vacs. Oh my, it's kitchen girls we need, not land girls. Oh my, oh my!

Sunday 12th Nov   THEY'VE ARRIVED!

Ooh, there've been some doings up at the big house! Cook put Lilly and Nessy – that's the land girls – to sleep upstairs next to Miss Joan; then Mrs Mole came home and had a fit – "Workers in the bedroom!" They've got to sleep over the stables and it'll be flipping freezing. The vacs say Cook has very red eyes.

Red with anger or red with tears? That's the question.

Frost patterns

Thursday 16th November
THE BIG FREEZE!

If this war don't end soon those land girls will freeze to death for certain – or Cook'll murder 'em! She gives them breakfast with the vacs, then they gets a paste sandwich and a flask of Bovril for their lunch and that's it; they ain't allowed in again until the evening meal! I don't blame her, she has no help and has to feed all them extras! What's more, Uncle C and Bathgate said they think women should keep off their land and out of their stables.

WAR EXTRA!
Two land girls have been found frozen in their beds. Police will not be able to identify the bodies until the ice surrounding them has melted. A Mrs Mouldy has been held on suspicion of deliberate cruelty. A local witness is understood to have said "Oh my, oh my, oh my!"

Fri 17th November '39

It was so cold in bed last night that me and Tommy was shivering – poor Dad, I bet he's shivering too. There's no more wool and I needs to make him and Tommy warm scarves.

Saturday 18th November

Lilly and Nessy seem to be winning Bathgate and Uncle C around. They work ever so hard and tonight they're taking the old codgers to the King's Arms. They'll have them purring in no time!

Later Dear Diary, I'm in the granary and it's freezing, but I wanted some peace from Tommy and to look for my mouse. He don't seem to be here. Maybe he's hibernating.

The blanket is still here. I think it's Simon's. I saw Molly spit at him yesterday and call him a "Nazi". Well he may be German, but he's no Nazi. I'm going to watch out for him.

I likes a
dropped
scone
or two.

Little pig!

A baby Austin

Honk,
honk!

Some of
Lilly and
Nessy's jobs

Muck out
the stables.
Feed, groom
and water
all horses.
Attend to
the welfare
of all estate
animals.
Mend gates,
fences and
hedges. Chop
logs. Prune
fruit trees.
Mind the
veg patch,
sweep the
yard, etc,
etc!

A SUNDAY TREAT!

Sunday 19th November 1939

I think Uncle C's worried about
Simon too. He's had him chopping
logs all afternoon and he brought
him in for his tea and made
drop scones! Tommy ate twenty!

Sunday 26th November

Miss Joan gave Tommy and me a
lift back from church in her little car. We freewheeled
most of the way to save her petrol ration. She says
she'll join the WRNS, that's the Women's Royal Naval
Service, if the war don't end soon. I'd like to join,
but Miss Joan says I must keep writing my diary and
bring Tommy up to be a brave boy instead!

Weds 13th December   COLD, COLDER, COLDEST

Bathgate let Lilly take us to school in the trap, but
halfway there she had to unhitch Trixie – the lane
was too icy – and we cut across the fields. Everything
was frost-white.

The milk was frozen at break, so we left it
by the stove until later
but then Miss Duncan
decided to send us all
home early. Tommy and me
have chilblains and pink
noses, but Miss D gave me
a couple of old sweaters to
unravel, so at least I can
knit them scarves.

His bottle will
have to go.

14th December — I GUESSED RIGHT AND SIMON TALKS!

Dear Diary, Last night I crept out to the granary and there was Simon. The poor mite was crying under his blanket and some old straw. He'd heard a noise and thought the Jerry had come for him. He says Maggie and Molly call him "a peeing Nazi", 'cos it's him as wets the bed. They're daft — Hitler wouldn't want no Jewish boy in his flipping party.

Simon said he'd show me a secret if I swore not to tell on him, so I swore. He opened his hand and there was MY Granary Mouse, living in his pocket. No wonder I couldn't find him! We're going to share him and call him Pocket! Then the blanket stirs and I find that Gracie's been sleeping with Simon too! Uncle C would have a fit; she should be guarding the chickens from foxes!

Where's that flipping dog?

I had to go back to bed, but I'm happy Simon and me is mates now. He speaks a bit funny, 'cos of his German accent, but he talks better than our Tommy!

Friday 15th December — LAST DAY OF SCHOOL!

Dad won't be home for Christmas. I'm that sad, but I _haven't_ cried.

Little goosey patter Be quick and get much fatter!

Sat 16th December 1939

I showed Dad's card to Cook and she gave me one of her massive hugs. She said it'll be a squash but we're all to have Christmas in her kitchen, and a goose and a bottle will help make things stretch!

Mrs Jones and her brat are off back to London today, so that's two less! She's never took to the country and there's been no bombs in London.

Mrs Rose is staying – Cook reckons she ain't got no family to go home to.

18th December

A Christmas card from Auntie Ethel and Frankie!
Uncle C's going to send them a chicken and some veg for Christmas, so Tommy and me have been decorating a box.

MERRY XMAS

MAY IT BE ALBRIGHT!

WARNING – HANDS OFF OUR TOMMY!

Tuesday 19th

Took the box over to Uncle Ron's for posting. Had lunch with him and Auntie Beth ... thought she might kidnap Tommy, so left early!

Sunday 24th December 1939   A GRAND NIGHT!

EVERYONE had the afternoon off: Uncle C, the land girls, Bathgate, the vacs, Cook and ALL – WE HAD SO MUCH FUN!

34

Cook gave us hot cocoa
and Christmas cake – I do
love Cook – then we wrapped up warm,
lit some lanterns and set off for the
village. It had snowed during the night
so we threw snowballs and at the top of
Drag Hill, we all squashed onto toboggans and flew
down to the King's Arms, arriving in a pile of giggles!

We had hot punch and mince pies, and then went
carol singing to raise money for the war effort. It was a
laugh – the whole village was out singing so all the houses
were empty! Simon, being Jewish, didn't know no carols, no
more did Maggie and Molly – and they ain't got no excuse!

Then we went to church for more carols and prayers for peace.
Each adult pulled a toboggan of children home; I think Uncle C
must have carried Tommy and me up to bed, I don't remember.

CHRISTMAS DAY 1939

Dear Diary, Happy Christmas to you! This has been a right
special day – I'm going to have to write pages!
Tommy was up with the dawn – he was that excited!
Father Christmas had been in the night
and we had an apple, nuts and sweeties
in our socks!

APPLE!

NUTS!

SWEETIES!

Happy
Xmas
to
Mum
and
Dad,
wherever
you are!
xxx

We tumbled downstairs to tell Uncle C and there was SIMON lying head-to-toe with him, and his sock was full too! I did hug Uncle C. Seeing Simon in out of the cold was next best to having Dad home. I wonder how Uncle C knew he slept in the granary –
I DID NOT TELL!

I won't have that dog or that mouse in the house, Christmas or no!

I found mouse prints in the dripping, but I don't think they was Pocket's.

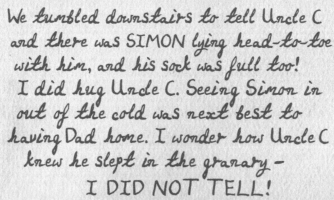

BREAKFAST

Fried bread
2 eggs EACH!
Tea with SUGAR!

PRESENTS...YES...PRESENTS!

Uncle C had carved Simon and Tommy wooden planes.
Him and Cook had made me a doll. I'm calling her Henrietta.

I'd decorated Uncle C a tin for his humbugs and Tommy gave us all a kiss! Simon said he hadn't known about presents, or that he'd have a Christmas-celebrating family, so his gifts would be late. That made even Uncle C well-up!

KEEP OUT

Q. Was it a Nazi that hid in the bakery over Christmas?

A. No, it was a mince spy!

DINNER   It was 4 o'clock by the time Cook finished serving lunch in the dining room, but we didn't mind. Lilly and Nessy made her sit down and they served everything. They'd even bought crackers with party hats and jokes.

When we ate Dad's goose we sang "For he's a jolly good fellow", which he is! The pudding had a peace flag on it and Uncle C sent it up in flames with the brandy!

Vera Lynn sings this song on the radio –
she's Dad's favourite!

SINGING, DANCING AND SPEECHES

We all helped clear away... even Tommy and
Mrs Rose. Uncle C gave a speech thanking
Cook, and Bathgate thanked the land girls –
Lilly hugged him and he blushed scarlet!
Then Uncle C got out his accordion
 and we all sang and danced.
We felt like one big family.

We'll meet again,
don't know where,
don't know when...

BOXING DAY 1939

Mrs Mole came to the cottage
to give Uncle C his Christmas box and a whole tin of mince pies. He didn't
let on how much he got, but he gave me, Tommy AND Simon sixpence each.
He told Simon he was to stay with us until his mum and dad came for him.
He said not to chat about it, because moving evacuees around ain't allowed.

 Simon told me that just before our Christmas, Jewish people celebrate
Hannukah – a festival of lights – and give each other presents. His mum
and dad must really be
missing him. He says he thinks
of his family every day, just
 like I think of my mum and
dad. He drew me a picture of
his family waving goodbye to
 him at the station.
 I promised I would always
keep it safe – and I will.

THE END
OF 1939

Mutti

Vati

Schwesterchen

This is Hebrew for "peace"!

37

WHIFFS

NO POOS

EARTH CLOSET

Uncle C has banned all poos, because he can't dig the icy ground to bury 'em.

Tommy ate his toast upside down!

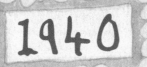

1940

Monday 8th January 1940   EVEN THE DUCKS ARE SKATING!

I don't reckon we'll be going back to school tomorrow – it's flipping freezing! We tried to make a Hitler snowman like Dad, but Tommy got too cold. Me and Simon made him toast and scrape and hot cocoa. Later Uncle C roasted some chestnuts he'd found. What a treat!

Tuesday 9th January 1940   WAR TALK

Lilly took us to school on the general's big hunter, Shannon, so no bunking off for us, worse luck. Miss Duncan talked about the war. She was that serious – even Tommy kept quiet. I've tried to write down what she said:

Germany

Austria

Czechoslovakia

Poland

Soviet Union

After the Great War, all the countries involved were very poor, but Germany suffered most. Now, Hitler and his Nazi party want to make Germany so powerful they'll never be defeated again. Over the last few years they have taken the Rhineland, Austria and Czechoslovakia! Nobody stopped them because nobody wanted another war. Then Hitler invaded Poland, but France and Britain had promised to help them and so we declared war on Germany.

The British Dominions are supporting us, but Ireland isn't. Luckily, I don't know no Irish people to be cross with, except the smithy and he's top brass!
The Soviet Union made a pact with Germany and by last October their armies had taken Poland and split it between them. Anyone who resisted was killed, including hundreds of Jews. It was too quick and too far away for us to help, but some Polish soldiers escaped into France and will continue the fight.

RUSSIA AND GERMANY SHARE OUT POLAND

Labels on map: Baltic Sea, GERMANY, Warsaw, German Soviet Line, POLAND, U.S.S.R, Brest-Litovsk

Together we can do it

Bien Sûr

Miss Duncan said it is not a "phoney war"! In the spring, Hitler will rearm and be on the move again. We shouldn't be scared, because Britain is an island and that makes it safer, but we should always BE ALERT!

Simon asked about his family and Miss Duncan said she'd heard rumours that Jewish families had been moved to camps, where they were working for the German war effort.

Simon says he hopes there'll soon be a thaw, so that the British Expeditionary Forces can march into Germany and rescue his family. I hope so too, and I think my Dad's just the one to do it, and to rescue the poor Polish people. <u>Message to Mr Hitler</u> – don't you be thinkin' you can have Britain too –

BECAUSE YOU CAN'T!

Please, Miss...

Maggie and Molly asked if they could go home to their Mam. Miss D said, "Not just yet, my lovelies!"

Please, Miss...

We was sent home at lunchtime on account of the weather. We slid home on the icy lanes. Simon and me had to try and hold Tommy, Maggie and Molly up ... impossible! We was like little icicles with wet bums!

A PRAYER
Please let Tommy learn to be good, Simon find his family, my dad stay safe and my mum be happy in heaven. Amen

Cook took us into the kitchen to warm up and to give me the BAD NEWS: Butter, sugar and bacon have all been rationed and I have to fetch our ration books from Auntie Beth's shop tomorrow.

Hands off my cheese!

When we got home Lilly was mucking out the stables in her gas mask!

MY DOLLYS
RATION BOOK

This is Henrietta's ration book! I wonder if the fairies have them.

Weds 10th January 1940   RATION BOOKS AND THE SHIVERS

More snow, so no school, but I did collect our ration books. They're full of coupons and when they run out... you starve! The Government says to cook more porridge ... flipping nuts! My lot only eat porridge with a ton of sugar and dobs of butter!

Pocket is with Simon day and night now, 'cos the granary's too cold. Imagine if Uncle C knew! I reckon Simon will smuggle Gracie in as well soon!

PAGE 18
34 BACON & HAM   34 BACON & HAM
33 BACON & HAM   33 BACON & HAM

We're house pets now – pass the sugar!

I got a cough and tonight I got the shivers, so I'm up in bed writing by candlelight. We've run out of paraffin for the lamps on account of the freeze. Tommy's got a cough too, poor mite.

I DON'T LIKE IT!

I found this under my pillow!

Flossie Here's a magic wishing acorn, and we's wishing you'll be well soon. Your fairy friends x

Sunday 28th January   18 DAYS LATER

It's weird... I woke up this morning in Uncle C's cot! Simon and Tommy were hanging over steaming bowls of balsam and Uncle C was making bread – Mum always said his bread had more garden muck than flour in it!

Soon as I tried to sit up I started coughing, but everyone cheered! It seems we've all had the whooping cough, but I was took really bad. The doctor couldn't get through the snow, so Uncle C's been nursing me, bless him.

Cook told him our room was a disgrace, so he moved me and Tommy downstairs. He's alone under the leaking roof now, but come spring the land girls will mend the thatch. Then the boys will move up there and I'll have the downstairs to myself! I'll be like a flipping princess!

feather – worm – muck more muck

Uncle C's bread

← No peas under my mattress, please!

Sunday 11th February   A IS FOR ARCHIE!

The snow has thawed, but all that whooping leaves you fair whacked so I can't go back to school! Tommy's stuck at home with me, so we're making alphabet cards. I think he's too young for his letters, but he's trying. I'm stuck on "X"!

Simon says he'll teach Tommy his numbers, 'cos he loves them! He's back at school ... with Pocket! Gracie has taken to following him there of a morning and then fetching him home. Uncle C says Simon should be a vet – he has such a way with animals.

  Secret: Simon told me that when I was really ill, Uncle C put Gracie up on my bed, so's she'd wake him if I got really bad – he's a one!

Monday 12th

Dad down a bunker!

I ♥ MY DAD

We got this letter from him today! He wasn't told I'd been poorly, on account of not worrying him!

Thursday 21st March

MY BIRTHDAY

The Easter holidays have started, which means I've missed a whole term of school! But I didn't whoop once this morning, so we had tea in the orchard. Uncle C made his garden-bread and Uncle Ron brought over homemade jam and clotted cream. Who needs their butter ration!

A is for Archie, our military pa.

B is for barrage balloons, floating afar.

C is for the colonel who gave you a ride.

D is for danger, so you better hide.

E is for the evacuees, our very good friends.

F is for the farmers, on whose food we depend.

G is for gas masks, and they ain't no fun.

41

H is for Hitler and horrid and Hun!

I is for Ireland, who won't help the fighting.

J is for Miss Joan, the cause of this writing.

K is for King George, who always does right.

L is for land girls, pretty and bright.

M is for military so willing and brave!

N is for the Navy, riding each wave.

I hope it don't make me look and behave like Auntie Beth!

Auntie Beth has cut down one of her old dresses for me; it's ever so pretty. Cook made me a cake, the vacs saved me their weekly sweets and Simon gave me a picture with a Jewish blessing. Tommy gave me a promise to "be gooder"!

A blessing for Good Tidings

Blessed art thou, O Lord our God, King of the universe, who art good and dispensest good.

Humph ... I know his promises. This morning I found all his crusts in the kitchen drawer!

Miss Joan brought me a NEW paint box for decorating my diary. She's off to join the Women's Royal Naval Service on Monday!

She's had a meeting with a First Officer and will probably be posted near here, but new recruits has to go to Plymouth first.

She says the Germans will soon be on the move again. She's going to send me all her war news for my diary. Ain't that grand! No birthday card from Dad, but I expect he's ever so busy.

Saturday 23rd March
YES! This beautiful card came from Dad today. **It's the tops!**

Dear ^neglected diary, I really feel better today and I ain't going to neglect you no more. I'll do some more knitting, in case the war lasts another winter. I'll get strong enough to go back to school, and I'll teach Tommy his letters and to be kind to animals. He held Ginger upside down over the pond this morning ... he said he was helping her fish!

Me: You promised you'd be good.

Tommy: Your birthday gone now!

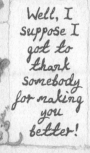

A lady thatcher is mending the cottage roof. It was too much for the land girls to fix.

Sunday 24th March 1940
EASTER DAY!!

I wore my new dress and we had decorated eggs for breakfast.
Then we all walked to church in the warm sun, even Uncle C.

I put daffodils in the boys' caps and primroses in my hair – we looked grand. The vicar gave us each a chocolate, but I gave mine to Mum – and the primroses. We had lunch at the pub as a special treat. I longed to hear the general's car coming around the corner carrying my dad, but I never did.

Uncle C walking to Church ↓

Well, I suppose I got to thank somebody for making you better!

We heard loads of lambs though. Tommy pretended each bleat was a bomb and kept diving under the table – we ignored him!

Even though it was Easter day there were loads of planes in the sky.

O is for the owl that made Simon sad.

P is for the postie, who brings letters from Dad.

Q is for queen, and I'd crown dear Cook!

R is for regiment, and it's to the Dorsets we look.

S is for sailors, who send messages by Morse.

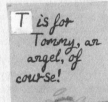

T is for Tommy, an angel, of course!

U is for an Uncle that is loving and fun.

Monday 25th March 1940

When I woke this morning Miss Joan had already left for Plymouth. I walked up the drive with Tommy and Simon to pick some flowers for Mrs Mole. Then, at the start of the lane, we spies Miss Joan's car parked right bang in the middle, so you can't pass on either side. Under the windscreen wiper there was a note for Bathgate, which I had to read to him. He said it was because his glasses were broke, but I reckon he can't read!

V is for the victory we're hoping will come.

W is for winter, which keeps the Hun quiet.

Bathgate

Car

Hedge

His missus gave me this

Bathgate

SIMON AND ME THINKS THE GROWN UPS KNOW THAT THE GERMANS ARE ABOUT TO INVADE US, BUT JUST AREN'T TELLING!

Thurs 4th April

Back to school today - it was great! The colonel had us digging up the playground for vegetables - you'd have thought we'd joined the army. He said to Tommy, "Fall in, young Albright, or I'll have you up before the general." You should have seen Tommy move!

PEAS   BEANS   ONIONS   RADISHES   LETTUCE   SPINACH   CARROTS

Our new skipping rhyme!

Run, Hitler, run, Hitler, run, run, run.
Don't give the Allies their fun, fun, fun;
They'll get by
Without their Hitler pie,
So run, Hitler,
run, Hitler, run, run, run!

<u>Later</u>: Uncle C has taken to listening to the 6 o'clock news on Cook's wireless. Cook reckons the whole country is sat listening! This evening, Uncle C was ever so quiet when he got back. He snapped at Tommy, just for dropping his spoon.

I <u>definitely</u> think the Germans is on the move!

Just for laughs, Cook's also been listening to Lord Haw Haw on the radio telling us to give up fighting. Not likely! We ain't cowards. Lord H used to live in England, so he's a big time traitor!

Jairmany calling, Jairmany calling!

WANTED DEAD OR ALIVE: ADOLF HITLER, WORLD ENEMY NUMBER ONE

<u>9th April 1940</u>   I WON'T LET MR HITLER SCARE ME!

The Germans have invaded Norway and Denmark – everyone is jumpy. Uncle C has mended the dodgy leg of our kitchen table. He says we're to hide there if German bombers come and we can't get to the big house. Tommy thought it was a lark, but Simon turned that grey colour again. I don't see as a table's going to save us from the Hun. I hope they don't invade us!!

ALL DENMARK OCCUPIED WITHOUT RESISTANCE

INVASION LIKE CLOCKWORK : ENTRY AT SIX POINTS

AMSTERDAM, Tuesday.
Germany's attack on Denmark and Norway to-day was carried out with a clockwork precision which bears witness to excellent staff work and careful preparation over a period of many months.

Boom, boom!

I'M SCARED!

Chamberlain
v

Churchill
From Miss
D's paper

Monday 22nd April 1940   THIS WAR IS NOT PHONEY!

Things ain't good. Miss Duncan says Germany is beating Norway, and Denmark didn't even try to fight. She thinks Mr Chamberlain is feeble and that Mr Winston Churchill would soon send Hitler packing if he was Prime Minister. I wish one of them would, 'cos we're awful close to the coast if we're invaded. I'm shaking at the thought – even though Tommy's got a proper gasmask now.

← I found these flowers today – the barks is a spring picture!

Tues 23rd April 1940
A cheering letter! →

Tomorrow Uncle C and Uncle Ron are going to try and shoot a fox and some crows that are taking the lambs. The farm dogs will be glad of the fox meat, but I'm NOT eating crow – war or no war!

A LETTER FROM MISS JOAN THE WRN!

A W.R.N.S. BADGE

Weds 24th April   FLIPPING UNCLES!

The wily old fox got away, but Uncle C bagged 6 crows. He says Simon and Tommy can help pluck them and then I'm to cook 'em. He'll be flipping lucky!

Eat us?
Cor, cor!

CROW PIE

Hang your crows for easy plucking, then gut and boil them. Lay the flesh on pastry; cover with herbs, gravy and mixed veg; cover with more pastry. Pinch, prick and glaze, then bake until golden brown.
      Try not to be sick when eating!

CARRION CROW AND YOUNG.

I'M NOT COOKING THEM AND THAT'S THAT!
Uncle C shot the flipping things – he can cook 'em.

One crow
for sorrow,
2 for joy,
3 for a
letter,
4 for a boy!

Sunday 28th April 1940   OH, DIARY!

When we got back from church, Uncle C was cooking crow pie! He said, "You kills things to eat or not at all and you don't waste food when there's a war on."

We all turned green. →

The pastry was full of garden muck and the crow made us retch.

Friday 10th May ⭐⭐⭐

PHEW!   NO CROW PIE TODAY

We had tea with Cook and listened to the news – it was terrible. We was all close to tears.

THIS IS FLOSSIE ALBRIGHT WITH THE BAD NEWS!
German panzers have crashed into Holland AND Belgium. They are rapidly crushing all resistance. Mr Chamberlain has resigned as our Prime Minister and the King has asked Mr Churchill to form a new government.

Miss D will be happy about Mr Churchill, but I don't see as one man can make much difference. Them German panzers must be awful close to Dad – he may even be fighting them at this very minute. Uncle C says   DAD! →

Dad is too soft, so how's he going to kill a man, even a German one? We might all be killed soon – no flipping kitchen table will save us from panzers.

I've written to Auntie Ethel, asking them to come here with Gramps. It'll be a squash, but I think it's best to face the dangers with your family. Simon cried when I said this, but we're his family now – only I'm supposing we ain't quite the same as the real thing.

DOUBLE, DOUBLE, SECRET!   NO ENTRY!

Saturday 11th May 1940

We all helped Uncle C today, even Tommy, Maggie and Molly. I pricked out the sweet pea seedlings, while the others planted sprout and cabbage plants. Tommy only threw earth at me once; Dad would've been proud of him. We all hope the veg'll be eaten by us and NOT the HUN!

cabbage

sprouts

Sweet pea seedlings

Bombs away!

← Gracie helped dig!

It's got to go!

Later Uncle Ron walked over with a rabbit pie for our tea. I gave him my letter for Auntie Ethel to post and some more socks for Dad. Uncle C put some baccy in one and Tommy put a picture of him feeding the ducklings in the other. I had to write "Tommy's being gooder" on it. Well, it ain't no fib, mostly!

I hope he's allowed stripy socks.

Hop — Jump — Dive — Vanish and Skipper

There's five ducklings so far – they're ever so sweet, and we've given them all names.

Weds 15th May 1940

Uncle C went to a meeting at the King's Arms, along with Bathgate. They are now members of the <u>Local Defence Volunteers</u>, or the Home Guard, as they're nicknamed. They're meant to be between 17 and 65 years, but some lads of 14 turned up with bows, arrows and broom handles – at least our heroes had guns and walking sticks! Now they've got tin helmets as well and Bathgate has got two gas masks for the horses – in case they're needed to defend their country. Uncle C is chuffed to be doing something useful, in spite of his age and gammy leg. These are his first orders:

Eh... what's that, you can see a Hun?

No, I said, ain't this fun!

OUR DEFENDERS!

WATCH OUT FOR SPIES

IF ANYONE ASKS FOR DIRECTIONS, SEND THEM THE WRONG WAY.

ALWAYS BE ALERT.

BY ORDER OF YOUR LDV

YES, SIR!

Quack!

Thurs 16th May

A heron took one of the ducklings — Jump, I think.

The evidence

US — THEM!

Monday 20th May

I think them flipping Germans have won. Miss Duncan says they've pushed right across France to Abbeville — they've reached the ENGLISH CHANNEL!

The Belgians have given up fighting and the French and British troops are trapped in the north of France, near Dunkirk. My dad might already be dead, or he might be cornered by the Germans and forced into the sea to drown. Then we won't have no army to stop the Hun invading England. Oh, poor us, and my poor, poor dad. Mr Hitler is a terrible man and whatever the vicar says I ain't never going to forgive him.

Tues 21st May

The flipping sun shone today — how could it? Did it shine on Hitler? I found this picture of → him and his dog — if I was his dog I'd run away so as not to be stroked by his wicked hand.

Simon has gone all grey and quiet again. How can we save his family when we can't even save ourselves?

"Draw a line under it and start again." That don't work when there's a war on — war changes everything, even if you don't want it to.

Simon's lamb

Weds 22nd May   SIMON'S BIRTHDAY!

Dear Diary, Uncle Ron brought over a late orphan lamb for Simon to hand rear! You should've seen his face — even when we told him about the night feeds he was grinning like a daft biscuit! Molly and Maggie offered to help and that's a first — Cook nearly fainted!

The lamb has to be fed <u>6</u> times day and night for the first week, then 4 times a day for 6 weeks. We had cake for Simon's birthday tea.

Drama: Tommy's had to give up his bottle to the lamb. Waaah!

Sat 25th HITLER HAS STARTED TO BOMB US

We didn't see the bombers fly over, but the first German bombs since 1918 have fallen in Essex and Yorkshire, injuring eight people. Simon has a lamb and a mouse inside his shirt now, and Gracie at his heels. Uncle C says he might as well not have a dog for all he sees of her. Tommy's no longer being "gooder" – he's

that cross the lamb has his bottle. Uncle C says to be patient, but he ain't with him all flipping day.

GOOD BOY!

Miss D ain't noticed lambkin yet!

Sun 26th May 1940 THE GRAMPS GUARD!

This Home Guard thing has gone to Uncle C's head! Him and Bathgate searched all the outbuildings for German spies this morning, and gave us an armed escort to church. The Gramps Guard – as Simon calls 'em – were so slow we missed half the sermon! And you can guess where they was waiting for us after church – the King's Arms!

Keep alert!

Not too much noise in the ranks!

Secret:

Strange

I'm not allowed, but I'm that worried, I went to ask Mrs Mole if she had news of Dad or the general. She said they'd soon be home, but I could tell she was close to tears. She gave me 6d for sweets, but I'm going to buy Dad something. I took Tommy up on Merry Hill to see if there were any ships coming back from France, but there wasn't a ship to be seen from Weymouth to Portland – there weren't even any fishing boats. Maybe they're in hiding because the Germans are about to invade us.

Not a boat or a ship to be seen!

Monday 27th May

Simon's lamb nearly died in the night. I woke to find Simon rubbing it with a towel and breathing into its little mouth. I fetched Uncle C and he gave it a slurp of apple brandy — it did the trick!

   I keep rubbing my lucky acorn and praying for peace.

Brandy always brings you round

Sunday 2nd June 1940

It was so quiet walking to church, we was all a bit spooked. Then the vicar told us that the church bells wouldn't ring again until the war was over or the Germans had landed. We'd been missing the sound of the bells!

The silent bell

Our village church

SURE MY DAD WILL FIND HIS WAY HOME TO ME!

Dunkirk

Abbeville

LATER   It kept churning inside me that Dad might already be in Dorchester, so I left Tommy with Simon and snuck out of school. I was dead scared walking out of the gates, but I had to find Dad. When I reached Dorchester I was that shaken — tired and dirty soldiers lay everywhere. Some of them had just fallen asleep at the side of the road and many were wounded and had lost bits of uniform. I ran to The Keep and my heart fair pounded as the duty sergeant looked down the list of soldiers who'd arrived back, but there was no Archie Albright.

Have you seen my dad?

I went on to the railway station; it was packed with people cheering, waving and handing out comforts to the soldiers. Trains came through the station every few minutes, but none of them let my dad off. When it started to get dark the Station Master tried to send me home, but I wouldn't go.

I waited all night and by morning I was shivering with cold and damp, but when I looked at the wounded soldiers asleep on the platform, I felt ashamed. I took Mrs Mole's 6d and bought a few buns and a jug of tea for some of them.

Then, all of a sudden an arm went around me and I nearly jumped for joy – but it weren't Dad – it were Uncle C come to fetch me. He wrapped me in his coat and hugged me tight and then he put me up on Trixie and set off home. I put my head down on Trixie's neck, buried my face in her mane and cried like a baby. I wanted my dad back so much it hurt.

Cheers, love!

Wednesday 5th June

DUNKIRK EVACUATION COMPLETED

I tore this bit of Mr Churchill's speech from Cook's paper. He really cheers me up!

down then ha... son, aiding each other like good comrades to the utmost of their strength. Even though large tracts of Europe and many old and famous States have fallen or may fall into the grip of the Gestapo and all the odious apparatus of Nazi rule, we shall not flag or fail. We shall go on to the end, we shall fight in France, we shall fight on the seas and oceans, we shall fight with growing confidence and growing strength in the air, we shall defend our Island, whatever the cost may be, we shall fight on the beaches, we shall fight on the landing grounds, we shall fight in the fields and in the streets, we shall fight in the hills; we shall never surrender, and even if, which I do not for a moment believe, this Isla...

Uncle C kept me home from school today; he said he needed help in the garden. Gracie stayed with me, and Lambkin, who's ever so strong now. When Simon got home he had a note from Miss Duncan. I thought it might say she wouldn't have me back no more since I run off, but Uncle C just stuffed it in his pocket and said he'd be back for his tea. Then he donned his tin hat and set off in the trap, so we got the tea ready and waited. We was all hungry and very jumpy; I had to slap Tommy's hand to keep it off the bread. It was hours before we heard Trixie trotting back. I shifted the blackout and looked out of the window. I could just see a body lying in the back of the trap – I knew it must be Dad.

Get the tea, gal. I got home guard duty!

I tried to stop Tommy running out, but he was gone before I could grab him. I rushed after him and saw that my dad was sleeping ... just sleeping ...

HE WASN'T DEAD AT ALL!

He'd been landed down the coast at Margate, so it had taken him a while to get to Dorchester.

NO!

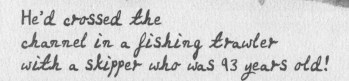

He'd crossed the channel in a fishing trawler with a skipper who was 93 years old!

Thurs 6th June 1940

NO SCHOOL AGAIN TODAY!

Dad slept right through to the afternoon, but when he finally woke, Cook came over to say she could smell him from the big house so she'd filled him a hot bath! Me and Tommy scrubbed the grime off his back, but we couldn't shift the bruises. After he'd had a shave and dressed in clean clothes, Cook gave us the best tea ever! Mrs Mole popped in and welcomed Dad home; she told us the general had been shot in the arm, but would be home in a day or two – we all cheered! Would you believe it ... my dad's home!!!!!!

MENU:
Sausages, mash, gravy, spring greens, bread, BUTTER, jam, tea and a beer for dad!

We'll have roast lamb on Sunday, to celebrate!

Said Cook

★ LATER ★ ★ ★ ★

I woke with a start in the night – it suddenly hit me – Simon had been missing since tea. I crept out to the granary and there he was, curled around Pocket, Lambkin and Gracie. I felt that stupid – I'd been so full of happiness at having my dad back, I'd forgotten he still had no news of his family.

Friday 7th June

Aye lad, it's only natural.

Said Dad

Dad walked us to school, so I told him that Simon was upset. Simon pinched me, but Dad understood. He said that the rescue from Dunkirk was good, but it wasn't a victory, so as soon as the soldiers had gathered their strength, they'd be back across the channel to sort out Hitler and his lot once and for all.

<u>At school</u> we saw that the carrots in the veg patch had come through, so Tommy pulled them up!
Miss Duncan laughed and said that they needed thinning, and we could replant them with the colonel. Miss D didn't laugh at me though. She said I done wrong to run off like that and give them all such a fright. She said next time I should talk to her first – then she gave me a hug. Dad collected us from school and took us to Auntie Beth's shop for a fizzy pop. She'd had a card from Auntie Ethel and a note from Frankie.

I felt this small.

Uncle C got an "invaders" leaflet at one of his Home Guard meetings. It's pinned up in the kitchen – it says that if the Germans invade we are not to tell them ANYTHING or give them ANYTHING, especially FOOD, MAPS or BIKES! Which ain't flipping likely as I don't have a bike!

Coz, Send some food, we's starving
...one is right tense now the
...based out of France.
..."...invader comes"
...send you one.
...we got loads
...sh them out.
...me, Frankie.

the bike!

THESE CERTAINLY ARE MOVING TIMES!

MABEL LUCIE ATTWELL

It don't say what you should do if they put a gun to your head.

<u>Mon... ...June 1940</u>   <u>Flossie's news special!</u>
Mr Mussolini of ITALY has declared war on BRITAIN and FRANCE. Dad says it's because he's a bloomin' coward and is sucking up to Hitler, because the Germans look like winning the war.

BUT YOU ARE MISTAKEN, ITALY –
THE ALLIES WILL WIN THE WAR!

I wrote notes to all my fairy friends and hung
them in the orchard – I hopes they find 'em.

11th June 1940   A BLACK DAY

My dad's gone again. I think he's gone to
help the French, because it said on the
news that the Germans are about to march
into Paris. I'm so scared. On a clear day you can see
France from the top of Merry Hill – it's that close.

18th June   This is what Mr Churchill said in the
← paper today ...

Please keep my dad safe.

Don't let us be invaded.

Let Miss Joan come home safe.

Don't let them bomb Frankie.

She don't want much, do she?

> The battle of France is over. I expect that
> the Battle of Britain is about to begin.
> Upon this battle depends the survival of
> Christian civilisation. Upon it depends our
> own British life, and the long continuity
> of our institutions and our Empire. The
> whole fury and might of the enemy must
> very soon be turned on us. Hitler knows
> that he will have to break us in this island
> or lose the war. If we can stand up to him,
> all Europe may be free and the life of the
> world may move forward into broad,
> sunlit uplands. But if we fail, then the
> whole world, including the United States,
> including all that we have known and
> cared for, will sink into the abyss of a new,
> Dark Age made more sinister, and perhaps
> more protracted, by the lights of pervert
> science. Let us therefore brace ourselves
> to our duties and so bear ourselves that if
> the British Empire and its Commonwealth
> last for a thousand years, men will say,
> "This was their finest hour".

Friday 21st
FRANCE HAS SURRENDERED!

Them flipping fairies can't read. We're all alone
now and I don't know where Dad is – he could be
a prisoner in France. What's more it's silage-
making time and the whole place stinks!

Saturday 22nd June

A card and a photograph from Miss Joan –
don't she look the business in her headphones!

The war news may be
bad, but I just noticed
something good: the vacs
have become countrified!
Even Simon's got pink
cheeks! They've been with
us nearly a whole YEAR!

Best wishes,
Miss Joan

Don't she look
a picture!

...ernie
...safely
...and in an
...up north
...rascal brother
...s a hug and
...one yourself,
...untie Ethel

MAGGIE

Before   After

MOLLY

Before   After

SIMON

Before   After

MRS ROSE & BABE

Before   After

Mon 1st July 1940

BARRICADING BRITAIN!

ANTI-AIRCRAFT GUN

PILLBOX

OBSERVATION POST

ARMY LORRY

GUARD POST

SYLVIA

BLUSHING →

We're not living in the country no more; we're living in a war zone. All day long, army lorries and jeeps rattle along the lanes. Uncle Ron says the noise is curdling his cows' milk. Soldiers are sticking poles in fields where German gliders might land, making tank traps and barbed wire barricades! Not to mention the anti-tank and aircraft guns, and the searchlights, pillboxes and observation posts being cemented on top of every hill.

Uncle Card Bathgate will have to man an observation post - I hope they remember their glasses and hearing aids or we won't get no warning of an invasion!

Auntie Beth says the shop is bustling with soldiers; Uncle Ron reckons it's on account of her new helper, Sylvia, who's as pretty as a daisy!

HITLER BEWARE - DORSET IS READY - INVADE US AT YOUR PERIL!

After school we took a flask of tea up Merry Hill and saw the barrage balloons glittering in the sun. We wondered if one of the battleships in Weymouth harbour was KGS with Miss Joan's friend aboard.

Then we rolled from the top of the hill to the bottom. Lambkin and Gracie chased us all the way; they go everywhere with us - I hate to think of Simon's face when Uncle Ron takes his lamb back.

PLAYER'S CIGARETTES

H.M.S. "NELSON"

A Battleship

Tues 2nd July 1940

Me and a mate at our station

NO ADMITTANCE

Dear Diary, I wish he hadn't mentioned my warts in front of Simon. Now he won't want to be my friend no more.

Wednesday 3rd July 1940
AIRCRAFT ALERT!

So many planes in the sky today! We think they're from RAF Warmwell, but I'm scared they might be German. There's talk that the Luftwaffe want to destroy our RAF – then they won't get bombed as they cross the Channel to invade us. We kept diving under hedges as we walked back from school. Simon says we got to learn our planes so we don't act silly. He's gone up to Uncle C's lookout post to copy down his aircraft chart.

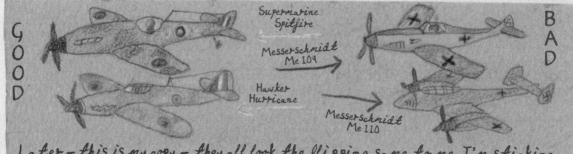

G O O D

Supermarine Spitfire

Messerschmidt Me 109 →

Hawker Hurricane

Messerschmidt Me 110 →

B A D

Later – this is my copy – they all look the flipping same to me. I'm sticking to hedges, 'cos I won't trust myself to know if a plane is friend or foe.

Thurs 4th July 1940   DRAMA IN THE SKY!

We saw great columns of black smoke rising into the sky over Portland way, so we went up on Merry Hill to get a better look and suddenly two fighters whizzed out of the clouds. The dogfight was so close you could almost see the pilots' whiskers. We was that caught up in it, we forgot to be frightened!

The German plane was hit and went down in flames. We saw the pilot bailing out and he was in flames too, but he landed too far off for us to help, so Simon ran to tell Uncle C.

Then I see a spitfire has been hit and the pilot is parachuting towards Tommy and me! Only a German plane comes out of nowhere and starts shooting at him and I could tell he'd been hurt.

He landed a few fields away so I ran to help him, dragging Tommy with me. Only he was dead when we got there, maybe his neck was broke, I don't know. Tommy took out his hanky and rubbed the pilot's brow and when that didn't work he tried kissing him better. I had to pull him off in the end and he had a huge howling fit. When he'd calmed down, we picked some flowers for the poor man and went to get help.

I carried Tommy and he fell asleep – then he woke up and was sick all down me. That's when I started crying for my mum – and for once I don't blame myself.

Sunday 7th July 1940

We heard today that the flaming German pilot survived. He'd knocked on a farm door over Chickley way, still in flames! Mrs Watts, the farmer's wife, threw a bucket of water over him and locked him in a barn. Then she fetched someone from the local defence and he was taken off in an ambulance. If he gets better, he'll be put into a prisoner of war camp and maybe help on a farm.

When in doubt, get the rolling-pin out!

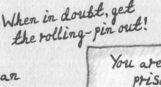

You are now my prisoner!

THE GREAT BRITISH FARMER'S WIFE

A BRAVE LADY!

59

Tues 9th July 1940

The Minister for aircraft production, Lord Beaverbrook, has asked us to give up our aluminium pans to help build more fighter planes. I only got one pan. I'm not sure I can manage without it.

Lord B

Dear Flossie,
We got your notes and we will keep our wings and wands on things. We sprinkled some fairy dust on you last night and you smiled in your sleep. xxx
Your Fairy Friends

A letter from the fairies at last!

We been designing posters to help our campaign.

THE COGS!

Help us to help our fighting forces - give us your old pots and pans and unwanted books and newspapers NOW! YOUR BUSY WAR WORKERS!

Weds 10th July BATTLING FOR BRITAIN

Dear Diary, <u>The Battle of Britain</u> has begun.
Flipping heck, I'm scared. I don't want to sleep all alone downstairs no more. The Luftwaffe has begun to attack British ships in the channel; our pilots spotted dozens of German aircraft dropping bombs on a convoy near Dover.
Cook says it's their invasion tactic to draw British planes into battle and then destroy them ... I hopes we got enough planes. I think the RAF may need my pan more than I do.

Thursday 11th July 1940

After school I went and asked Cook for some old pans. She gave me three! So me, Simon, Tommy, Maggie and Molly have joined the COGS CLUB. We'll get a badge if we collect enough aluminium. We might even help a pilot like the one on Merry Hill.

<u>BAD LOCAL NEWS</u> - Cook spotted my warts! She says I must rub the juice of a milk thistle on them every day for two weeks ... lovely!

Saturday 13th July 1940

We took Uncle C's wheelbarrow up to the village and filled it with scrap. Everyone wanted to help. Then we took it to the collection point and the warden (Uncle Ron!) told us if we kept it up, we'd be sure to get a badge ... it'll be like our very own war medal!

Hooray, hooray, it's the last day!

Tuesday 16th July 1940   LAST DAY OF TERM!!!

Tear up
your
books,

burn
your pens,

THIS IS
THE DAY
THE TERM
ENDS!!!!

In assembly, Miss Duncan gave us one of her war talks:

Listen up now, children.
She knows her stuff!

Tee-hee!

Tommy tried
to climb up
and nearly
pulled Miss D over!

Uncle C
calls him
"the old bulldog"

Remember – radar is our magic weapon! The steel masts you see along the coast are the "ears" of the radio direction stations. Controllers can hear the German bombers approaching and send our pilots out to fight them. (Miss Joan trains officers to do this!)

Remember – German planes take off from captured airfields in France, Belgium and the Netherlands so they soon run out of fuel. Our planes are close to home so they can fight for longer!

Remember – if we shoot down a German pilot, he will be taken prisoner. Our pilots are over home ground and can find another plane to fly!

Remember our allies! Many French, Polish and Czech soldiers and pilots escaped the Germans and are now in England preparing to fight beside our armed forces.

Remember – WE WILL WIN THE WAR!
Do not forget this during the holidays.

Then we had to learn these words of Mr Churchill's by heart:
The war will be long and hard. No one can tell where it will spread. One thing is certain: the peoples of Europe will not be ruled for long by the Nazi Gestapo, nor will the world yield itself to Hitler's gospel of hatred, appetite and domination ... But be the ordeal sharp or long, or both, we shall seek no terms, we shall tolerate no parley; we may show mercy – we shall ask for none.
PHEW – I was glad to get home!

He sounds
very brave.

61

We went on a beetle hunt and we found:

A Bumble-dor

A Green Tortoise Beetle

A Click Beetle

A Burying Beetle

Weds 17th July 1940

THE FIRST DAY OF THE HOLIDAYS

Dear Diary, I decided to have a muck about day – no housework and no flipping war talk! We had a picnic and swam in the stream. It was ripping, but it's almost impossible not to think about the war. If the Germans bomb Weymouth they might hit Honeysuckle Cottage by mistake.

Hee-hee

We tried to tickle some trout for supper... no luck!

WE ARE HITLER'S MAIN ENEMY NOW.

Sunday 21st July 1940

DAD BIKED OVER FOR THE DAY!!!!!!

We were up at Uncle Ron's helping with the harvest, when Dad arrived! We sat in the sun and feasted on bread, cheese and apple cider. There wasn't a fighter plane in sight. Oh it was grand, grand, grand! I can tell Dad EVERYTHING, he always listens.

He won't be over again for a bit, on account of the Germans keeping them on the hop with their raids.

Dad jumped out from behind the haycock!

Boo!

Tommy picked me an ox-eye daisy when Dad left, root and all! →
Uncle Ron said it was time to put Lambkin back with her flock. Simon was very brave, but I'm sure he thought Lambkin would chase after him. She seemed quite happy, though. I said it was 'cos he'd brought her up right!

Monday 29th July 1940

Too much work!

What with the harvest, cooking, cleaning, feeding the animals, watering the veg and teaching Tommy manners ... I ain't had much time to write.

TOMMY'S LATEST HORROR: A grass snake in the kitchen drawer!

Passsss the sssssssalt!

I BLAME SIMON FOR GIVING HIM THE WRETCHED THING.

Tuesday 30th July
THE FLIPPIN' HUN

Now the Germans are bombing our airfields and
Channel convoys day and NIGHT. Sometimes we
see our planes flying off to fight them, or spot
a puff of smoke out at sea as a bomb lands or a
plane goes down. The fishermen say the attacks
are killing loads of fish, so we soon won't have
no fish to eat. I'm thinking those without a
veg patch will starve. Uncle Ron has warned us
to be extra careful because as the German
bombers make for home, they're ditching leftover
bombs in the fields.

Still collecting scrap, nearly another barrow load!

No letter from Miss Joan. I reckon she's too busy
training them handsome officers on tricycles!

20th August
Cook insisted I
stick this cutting
in of Mr Churchill's
latest speech.

> Never in the field of human
> conflict was so much owed by
> so many to so few. All hearts
> go out to the fighter pilots,
> whose brilliant actions we see
> with our own eyes day after
> day; but we must never forget
> that all the time, night after
> night, month after month, our
> bomber squadrons travel far
> into Germany, find their targets
> in the darkness by the highet
> navigational skill, aim their
> attacks, often under the
> heaviest fire, often with serious
> loss, with deliberate careful
> discrimination, and inflict
> shattering blows upon the
> whole of the technical and
> war-making structure of the
> Nazi power.

Sat 24th August
Dear Diary, I'm sorry if
you feel neglected but like I said ... us kids is doing all the work
of the adults away in the forces. Cook's added making pull-
throughs (used by the soldiers for cleaning their gun barrels)
to my list of jobs – it's ever so easy. Cook and Simon
make fishing nets and
that's really tricky.

Cook always gives us a mug of
cocoa and a rock cake.

A pull
through!

I don't want
to miss no
schooling,
because I'm
thinking I
might want
to be a nurse.

Thursday 5th September
Went back to school today – none of the
farm kids turned up. I expect they're
helping out. Food's so short no one seems
to mind them missing school.

Tues 10th Sept 1940 — LONDON BOMBED!

We had this letter from Frankie and Auntie Ethel. London must be taking the worst of the war — the bombing sounds terrible. I reckon I'm lucky to still have family in London with so many killed and wounded.

Me and Simon — hindered by Tommy — drew this picture of how we think London must look.

Simon visited Lambkin today; she was busy cropping grass and ignored him. Simon went quiet, but when we got home he set Pocket free in the granary. I think he done right — things is happiest when they're free.

  FREEDOM!

Sunday 15th September 1940 — THE DANGERS OF GOING TO CHURCH!

No sign of Frankie and Ellie; I hopes they do come, squash or no squash. Our biggest danger comes from the Gramps Guard! They march about the lanes, helmets on and rifles at the ready, looking for spies. They even stopped us on the way to church and searched our prayer books for secret messages. They're flipping bonkers!

Cook says one HG officer shot himself in the foot while trying to arrest the smithy for spying! He'd joked about hiding messages inside a horse's hoof — what with that and his Irish accent, he was lucky not to be shot!

She don't like the HG around when I'm hiding the coded messages!

Mon 16th Sept 1940   THE STRETCHER PARTY!

Dear Diary, Some women from the WI are training as stretcher bearers. They say they can run two miles with a sixteen stone man!

KEEP UP THE PACE, GIRLS!

Well, this evening Auntie Beth agreed to be "the body" and they were running with her over the bridge when one of them slipped, and Auntie Beth went over the edge into the river! She arrived here dripping wet and spitting newt venom! This is the honest truth!

I'll put them in the mincer and sell them by the pound!

Friday 20th September 1940   THE INVASION!!!!

NB This may be my very last entry!   I'm ever so sorry I laughed at our Gramps Guard, because I'm glad of them tonight. We were having our tea, when the church bells rang out, signalling an invasion! Uncle C rushed to the lookout post and Bathgate is at the end of the drive. The land girls are guarding the front of the big house with Gracie, while we're all hiding in the cellar. It's right scary – we've only got the general's old tennis racquet to fight off the Hun. Luckily, Cook has brought provisions, but the vacs are still snotty about fruit!

Cook to Maggie: An apple a day keeps the doctor away.
Maggie to Cook: An onion a day keeps everyone away!

THE NEXT MORNING We're all bursting for the toilet! Cook has just put her nose out of the door and as it all seems quiet we are each scurrying to the bog and back. I could hardly go with the fear of it.

NEXT TIME, TAKE A BUCKET. FLIPPING HECK!
Bathgate has just come and given us the all clear.
IT WAS A FALSE ALARM, but the message has only just got through. Cook is making us a strong recovery brew and some dinner, so I better stop writing and give her a hand.

Mrs Mole joined us – stiff as a board, she is.

65

Good gracious, moo!

Is Nelly the first cow to produce exploding milk?

THANK YOU POSTIE!

Today we got a most excellent post – a COMIC card from Dad and a TOP SECRET letter from PETTY OFFICER Mole!

Friday 25th October 1940   WAR WORK FOR KIDS!

Dear Diary, Since Mum died, I've pretty much had to take care of things, but I ain't alone in that no more. The war has meant that loads of other kids is having to get stuck-in. Even school is different; we do as much war work as we do maths. Today we made war posters. These are mini versions of mine:

DIG FOR VICTORY

As well as caring for our playground veg patch, we are now digging up the village green ready for planting! The ducks is loving the mud and the worms.

JUST GIVE YOUR SALVAGE KIDS A SACK

We still collect aluminium and paper, but now we're collecting rubber-soled shoes for mending tyres and old tins, which Uncle C makes into mugs for people who have lost everything in the blitz.

They're a bit sharp around the edge!

AND SEE THERE'S PLENTY IN IT!

ACORNS NEEDED TO FEED LONDON ZOO'S ANIMALS

We're all collecting acorns for the animals. The Zoo has sent most of their animals up north, away from the bombs. (Except the bears, 'cos they hide in their caves if they hear a bomb coming!)

Any bombs?
All clear!

We sent Dad's presents to The Keep. I hope he got them. →

BLACKBERRIES

We pick and sell these to the smithy; he takes them to the Dorchester market. We bought Dad a comic and some barley sugar with the money.

Not that I've ever done no serious scrumping, not like some kids I know! →

NO SCRUMPING!

We ain't been scrumping this year, it don't seem right when food's so precious, but we did help the land girls pick and sort the orchard fruit.

Rosehip Syrup Recipe. Boil 2lbs of rosehips for 15 minutes in 3 pints of water. Drain through a jelly bag, then add a pint of boiling water, etc, etc!

MAKE ROSEHIP SYRUP BY ORDER OF THE MINISTRY OF FOOD. HARVEST THE HEDGEROW – IT'S RICH IN VITAMIN C!

I've made rosehip syrup; it's ever so tasty, but it don't keep long.

While we were making the posters, Miss Duncan and the colonel started to teach us some songs for a Christmas concert. We're learning a few carols, but mostly songs to cheer people up, like "We'll Meet Again", which Vera Lynn sings on Cook's wireless – it makes Uncle C swoon. The bombing in London is still very bad.

Miss Vera-make-you-Swoon Lynn!

Saturday 26th October   I DECLARE A DAY OF REST

– so go back to bed Mr Hitler, you can't do no fighting when Flossie Albright's sleeping. ♥ ♥ ♥ ♥ ♥

Sunday 27th October 1940   THE BEST OF DAYS!

DAD TURNED UP! He was waiting outside church with a big bag of clothes for us! A mate in his regiment said his kids had grown out of them – there's a warm cardigan for me and vests for everyone – ain't we lucky!

67

PS He had got his comic and sweets; he was ever so pleased.

Dad made Uncle C leave the King's Arms and come home so we could all sit down for dinner together. Tommy was on his best behaviour and we had a grand time. I thought Dad would go after tea... BUT HE'S STAYING THE WHOLE NIGHT!!

Home Guard, HOME. Quick march!

Monday 28th October 1940

Dad walked us to school, so as to be with us as long as possible and to thank Miss D for being so good to us. She blushed and said "just doing my bit". Then he gave us each a threepenny bit and a hug and was gone. I wonders and wonders – when will I see him again? Until you lose someone you love, I don't reckon you believe it's possible, but I knows it is.

Riches!

THREE PENCE 1940

MY DAD IN HIS UNIFORM

Friday 8th November IT'S FREEZING AGAIN!

The vile chilblains are back ... but no warts, thanks to Cook! I'm right glad of my new cardie and vest. We did school work this morning, but in the afternoon we went out with the colonel and collected wood for the school stove and for a couple of village oldies. Tommy collected so much the colonel said he should be promoted to sergeant!

Yuck! She's got red hair, red toes, red fingers AND WARTS!

Them warts is gone!

The rehearsals for our Christmas show are going well. Tommy is to be an angel ... ho, flipping ho! → Simon and me are going to dress as pixies and introduce the songs!

Monday 11th   FESTIVE WAR WORK!

We had a brilliant day at school! We started to pack <u>Christmas parcels</u> for the forces. We decorated boxes and filled them with things like ink, paper, bandages, soap, socks and sweeties, delivered to us by the WI.

You got to salute me now, I'm a Sargint!

Angel wings

Then we made a jolly card and tied up the box; it was really good fun! The boxes are going all the way to NORTH AFRICA!

SOCKS

SOAP

FIRST AID

SWEETIES

PEN

INK

PAPER

GLOVES

Miss Duncan told us that a lot of our supplies come from India and Burma and travel on ships through the Suez Canal and across the Mediterranean Sea. Ever since the Italians joined the war, they've been trying to capture the canal and cut off our supplies.

So North Africa and the Mediterranean Sea have become the biggest Theatre of War.

The Italians ain't doing too well because the British soldiers in Egypt have captured thousands of them and are driving the rest back into Libya. The Italians also tried to invade Greece, but the Greeks are pushing them back into Albania, while in the Mediterranean naval bombers are sinking the Italian ships. Sounds to me as if it's the Italians that need Christmas parcels, not the Allies!

us!

Albania

Black Sea

Greece

Mediterranean Sea

Suez Canal

India

Cairo

Algeria

Libya

Egypt

Tommy is now refusing to be an angel in the school show - he says the colonel, "'moted me to a sargint" - cheeky young tyke!

Don't be daft, bad news always travels.

Thursday 14th November 1940

Dozens of German bombers flew over today; I hopes they ain't heading for London. I wish Frankie and Ellie were here. We haven't heard a word since September – they could even be dead.

I had a card from Miss Joan with her unit on the front. It weren't really for me, but I suppose she felt it should go in the diary. She also sent a photograph of her boyfriend – he looks like a film star! Simon says he's got shifty eyes, but I think they're brooding!

Can you spot me?!

Speckington 1940

I'm going to copy out this letter for Mrs Rose's poor baby, because he won't ever know his Daddy.

Saturday 16th Nov 1940

Terrible news, them bombers were on their way to Coventry. 568 civilians were killed and the cathedral was destroyed.

That's 27 miniature gravestones – can you imagine what 568 real ones might look like?

A pint and a  packet of crisps!

I hope the Gramps Guard don't arrest them. There's no telling what they might do after a pint of cider!

Sunday 17th Nov 1940   TWO BAD PENNIES

I reckon Cook told Mrs Rose about her husband being a hero, because she kept sobbing in church. Afterwards, she and Cook went and joined the Gramps Guard at the King's Arms, so Maggie and Molly came home with us.

We'd just sat down for dinner when we heard a scuffling outside and Gracie, who was in by the fire, started to growl. We quickly locked the door and ducked under the table. We was dead scared, but after a bit Gracie stopped her growling and began to scratch at the door. So we opened it a chink ... and there lay Frankie and Ellie, shivering cold and fit to die with exhaustion! We dragged them inside by the stove and wrapped them in a blanket; Simon made hot cocoa and fried bread, while I tried to rub some warmth into little Ellie. She didn't half cry, poor mite, as her toes came back to life.

BEFORE

IF IN DOUBT WHO'S WITHOUT, ASK A DOG!

AFTER

I told you bad news always travels!

They'd been travelling for two days. They'd got on an early train to Dorchester on Saturday, and then they'd set out to walk here. Only what with the cold and the signposts pointing in the wrong direction, they'd got lost. Then it got dark as pitch and they couldn't find a place to shelter. I don't know why Auntie Ethel didn't ring the shop to tell us they was coming.

Uncle C was ever so pleased to see them, even though that's four in his bed! I'm that glad to have Ellie in with me, as long as her toes stay warm.

Uncle C growled at Gracie for being inside, but said nothing to Simon.

Icy rain all day.

Monday 18th November 1940

Dear Diary, Like my dad says, Miss Duncan's a good woman – she didn't bat an eyelid when we turned up with two extra! Frankie was really rude; he said he was "too bleedin' old for school", so Miss D asked if he would be her helper for 6d a week ... so then he burst into tears!

YOUR VILLAGE SCHOOL, ALL WELCOME!

It turns out they'd been bombed out of their house. Not a wall was left, not a stick of furniture, not their precious tins of food, not even Frankie's bike or Ellie's doll. Luckily, they'd all been in the street shelter, but since then they've been living in a school hall along with dozens of other homeless families. They might have been there for months; there are just too many people for the council to house. Frankie didn't even know how to contact Auntie Ethel to say they were safe. No wonder she didn't call the shop, and no wonder they had nothing with them.

WANTED
A KEY TO OUR OWN FRONT DOOR ANY SIZE, ANY SHAPE!
THE HOMELESS

Miss Duncan is going to contact the Salvation Army, and hopefully they will find Auntie Ethel and tell her the kids are safe. She thinks that the WI will find some clothes for them, and a camp bed for Dad when he's home, as five in the bed might be a bit much of a SQUASH!

AND A DOLL!

When we got home, Uncle C had made two extra chairs out of old apple boxes and two of his special "cut your lip" tin mugs. Cook had left a rabbit pie for our tea, bless her.

FLOSSIE, DON'T TELL MRS M. COOK

Secret: I gave Henrietta to Ellie, but don't tell, 'cos I don't want to hurt Uncle C's feelings.

AND NOW – HERE IS OUR VERY OWN FLOSSIE ALBRIGHT WITH THE NEWS.

Mr Adolf Hitler is thinking of invading his friend and ally, the Soviet Union. How would you like Adolf for your friend?

Thursday 19th December '40 — THE CHRISTMAS CONCERT!

Today was the last day of school and our Christmas show went with a BANG! Frankie helped Miss D with the props and Ellie dressed up as a fairy and introduced the acts with Simon and me. We all joined in the singing and "Sargint" Tommy recited a Ministry of Food nursery rhyme ... with a little prompting and a lot of saluting!

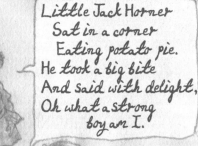

Little Jack Horner
Sat in a corner
Eating potato pie.
He took a big bite
And said with delight,
Oh what a strong
boy am I.

Ellie made a lovely fairy!

I was proud of him!

Bathgate brought Uncle C, Cook and Mrs Rose plus the nipper, in the trap. They'd all put on their Sunday best and Uncle C had combed his beard! I hoped and hoped that Dad might sneak in, but he must have been too busy. There was so much clapping at the end that I reckon if a bomb had dropped, we'd not have heard it! Why is it that I sometimes miss Mum most when things is at their best?

Christmas comes but once a year,
And when it comes it brings good cheer.
It brings us pudding, it brings us pies,
It brings us everything that's nice.

Friday 20th December

It snowed in the night, but the postie still came crunching down the lane. A Christmas card from Auntie Ethel and Gramps AND A COMIC CARD FROM DAD!

Christmas Greetings from the Fire Service

And Gramps

CHRISTMAS SPECIAL

POST EARLY FOR CHRISTMAS

Wacko Kiddos! Keep your eyes peeled for a Christmas Eve surprise! Dad. xx
PS Don't forget Ethel and Gramps at Christmas, ask Uncle C if we can spare a few rations for them again this year.

HAPPY CHRISTMAS

Christmas Eve 1940

We tobogganed into the village to sing carols, just like last year. The light of the moon on the snow made it seem bright as day. We'd have made lovely targets if there'd been a bomber about. I didn't spot Dad's surprise.

As usual, all us kids fell asleep on the way home and the grown-ups had to pull us on the toboggans. I opened an eye to thank Uncle C as he lifted me into bed, and realized – _it was Dad!_

IT WAS A WACKO CHRISTMAS EVE SURPRISE!

Christmas Day 1940

There were no oranges in our socks this year, but there were nuts, sweeties, a comic AND a three-penny bit. HAPPY CHRISTMAS WORLD, HAPPY CHRISTMAS MUM, HAPPY CHRISTMAS ALLIES AND EVEN ENEMIES. No time to write more, having too much fun!

Boxing Day 1940

THE BEST EVER – FLIPPING RIPPING!!!!!!!

I don't know where to start – it was ALL so exciting. Dad had to go back to The Keep, and Uncle C said we could take him in the trap along with Maggie and Molly. Bathgate wasn't happy on account of the ice, but Uncle C ignored him.

I'M SURE PEACE IS AROUND THE CORNER.

A NEW YEAR 1941

Wednesday 1st January 1941

Dear Diary, happy flipping miserable New Year. How wrong can your friend Flossie be? Answer: VERY! Peace ain't around the corner; not any corner as I can see. We didn't celebrate New Year because there was nothing to celebrate.

Here is the news with our very stupid Flossie Albright:

The Germans celebrated the end of 1940 by dropping incendiary bombs on London. People lost their lives and their homes. When Frankie heard, he wanted to go and help his mum fight the fires, but Uncle C wouldn't have it.

Thursday 9th January 1941
FIRST DAY BACK AT SCHOOL

In assembly Miss Duncan said we must "stick together and stick it out". Sounds like a flipping government war slogan.

DIG FOR VICTORY! — CARELESS TALK COSTS LIVES. — MAKE DO AND MEND. — LEND A HAND ON THE LAND! — WOMEN OF BRITAIN – COME INTO THE FACTORIES!

She also gave us a war lesson – I used to like them, but not today. Anyway, just for Miss Joan, here it is:

AT SEA

A lot of our new ships, planes and munitions are travelling across the Atlantic from the US. Although they are protected by British warships, the German submarines form "wolf packs" and try to torpedo them. They are quite good at it, but we're good at fighting back and the US is brilliant at supplying us with new ships!

WE NEED HELP!!!

The US gives us money and they build us ships, but they won't help us fight. How can a little island like ours keep the Germans out and win back our allies' land?

75

NORTH AFRICA

Help! Help!

The Italians are losing so badly to the Allies that Miss D reckons either Hitler will send help or the Italians will give up!

AT HOME

In spite of air raids and the threat of invasion, we are standing strong! We will stick together and stick it out!

I showed Miss D the alphabet cards I made for Tommy — she says to finish them and she'll use them in school...

X for an Xplosion of Xcitement!

Tommy knows at least six of his letters.
I reckon he's really clever, 'cos he ain't three yet!
OR I'M JUST A BRILLIANT TEACHER!

Y is for yours truly, the star of the team.

I hope Miss Joan's friend, Peter, don't get torpedoed.

I've been thinking: It could be that Mr Churchill is too proud, so maybe I should write to the US president, Mr Franklin Roosevelt, and tell him how badly we need his help.

Z is for zoo, our Simon's dream!

I finished 'em at last.

Saturday 1st February 1941

We don't want to go!

Mrs Rose and the nipper are to leave High Barn tomorrow. Mrs Mole has found her a job at the Old Soldiers' Home, in Dorchester. Mrs R is ever so tearful. We're all the family she's got now, but Mrs M says there'll be more life for her in Dorchester and she can visit us on her day off.
I reckon Mrs M just don't like having vacs around.

My dear, they make the place look so untidy!

Sunday 2nd February

After church, we went to the King's Arms for a farewell drink with Mrs Rose before Bathgate took her on to Dorchester. The land girls whooped with joy, because now they can move into her room — no more freezing to death above the stables.

DORCHESTER NEWS EXTRA 1d

TWO ICE-BLOCKS HAVE SUDDENLY THAWED, REVEALING...

BLUE NOSED LAND GIRLS

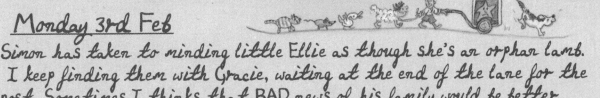

Monday 3rd Feb

Simon has taken to minding little Ellie as though she's an orphan lamb. I keep finding them with Gracie, waiting at the end of the lane for the post. Sometimes I thinks that BAD news of his family would be better than NO news, just so's he'd know. Is that a terrible thing to think? Frankie just wants to go back to London. He snaps at poor Tommy who thinks Frankie's the flipping tops ever since he helped to rescue us from that snowdrift.

Flipping kids!

Saturday 15th March

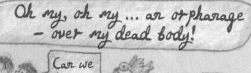

Dear Diary, I ain't written much because we been short on sunlight, candles and paraffin. Also, we've all been flattened by the terrible news that Maggie and Molly's mum has been killed in a bombing raid. Ever since the evacuee lady came to tell them, they've clung on to Cook's skirt like she might vanish too. She's that kind to them, but Mrs Mole says they'll have to move to an orphanage, as nobody seems to know where their dad is.

THERE AIN'T NOTHING WORSE THAN NOT HAVING A MUM.

Oh my, oh my ... an orphanage – over my dead body!

Can we keep us shoes?

Friday 21st March

Dear Diary, I just thought I'd give you the chance to say,

HAPPY ELEVENTH BIRTHDAY MY VERY GOOD FRIEND FLOSSIE!

That's the thing about diaries ... you 'as to listen really hard to hear 'em!

The orchard fairies painted me this lovely card! →

HAPPY BIRTHDAY FLOSSIE xxx

OUR COUSINS, THE BEETROOT FAIRIES!

77

Saturday 22nd March

As we had school yesterday, we celebrated
my birthday today. We picnicked in the meadow and made
a fairy scarecrow which made us all laugh.

We met the gypsies on the way home and Cook bought pink

ribbons for the girls' hair — just like she
promised nearly two years ago! Uncle C bought
me and Ellie sky blue ribbons and the boys
got lucky rabbits' tails. Then we chased
each other home. Poor Uncle C was slow and
wheezy as damp wood on a fire.

Secret: It's odd, but I'm so used to not having Dad around,
I didn't miss him until the evening. THEN I MISSED HIM LOADS!!!!

Gracie is going grey around the muzzle.
Simon says this is rot, but she is!

Good news: We ain't heard no more about
the two M's going to an orphanage.

Grey? It'll be wrinkles next!

Sunday 30th

Dear Diary,
Just because I ain't written much about the war, don't mean it's gone away.
To tell the truth, I can hardly face writing about it.
   Mr Hitler won't ever see the harm he's done to those two little girls by
killing their mum, or see Simon waiting in the lane for a letter that may
never come. I HATE HIM!!! AND I WANT MY DAD HOME.

31st March 1941   THE NORTH AFRICAN THEATRE

Miss D was right about Hitler sending the Italians some help in
   North Africa; he sent Lt General Erwin Rommel. His
Afrika Korps has already driven the British out of two
   towns in Libya. Rommel has been nicknamed the "Desert
Fox" on account of him being so cunning, but I think
            he looks more like a RAT. ———>

 Good evening, here is the BBC news.

And it ain't good.

Monday 21st April

Uncle C and Frankie still go to Cook's of an evening to listen to the news. Tonight Frankie tells me Greece and Yugoslavia have surrendered to the Germans and our troops are leaving Greece. Can I stop that? No. I would if I could and I <u>ain't</u> a whinger, but I just want my Dad home and to play with my mates – like the old days.

Cheep cheep!

Friday 24th April

OUR TWO-WEEK EASTER HOLIDAY STARTS HERE!

12th May 1941   TERRIBLE NEWS

The Germans have been bombing London for two days. The Houses of Parliament, Westminster Abbey and the British Museum have all been damaged – along with hundreds of homes. Frankie is frantic with worry about Auntie Ethel, but Uncle C has forbidden him to go back to London. We ain't had no news from Ethel since Easter and being in the Fire Service is really DANGEROUS!

Wacko, Flossie!

13th May   ♥ ♥ DAD CAME HOME! ♥ ♥

Surprise! Dad borrowed an army jeep and drove over to talk to Frankie and Ellie. If we don't hear nothing from Gramps and Auntie Ethel by the weekend, Dad will get a special pass and go up to London to look for them. Frankie's not going to let Dad go without him, that's certain. I ached when Dad went, but I didn't blub on account of not wanting to upset Ellie. Uncle C played silly songs on his accordion to cheer us up and we taught him a couple from school:

Whistle while you work!
 Hitler is a twerp
All his army
  Have gone barmy
Whistle while you work!

In 1941 old Hitler
ate a bun
He got an ache
Which made him quake
In 1941.

Zees must be zee British bun.

Friday 16th May 1941

Uncle Ron came over after tea with news from London. Gramps had phoned the shop to say he and Ethel were both fine and he'd send more news before too long. WHAT A RELIEF! Uncle Ron brought us some milk, butter and cheese ... ANOTHER RELIEF. It takes more than the food from a ration book to fill my boys.

Uncle Stinky Ron

Sorry lad, no lamb

Pong! I been muck spreadin'!

1 person's food ration for a week!

That's one egg too many!

| 4oz butter | 2oz tea | 4oz bacon | 1 egg | 1oz cheese | 8oz sugar |

21st May SIMON'S BIRTHDAY AND A LETTER FROM AUNTIE ETHEL

To celebrate the double good news I baked a cake after school.

To celebrate Simon's birthday, I got everyone to help decorate the orchard with garlands of flowers and coloured paper – even Frankie joined in! I delivered invitations to the fairies, too.

What, no fairy cakes?

How kind of you to let us come.

Uncle C sang us a song, Cook told us about getting caned at school for not knowing her sums,

Dear Flossie. Thanks for inviting us to Simon's tea party. You is a great little cake maker and our acorn teacups were just the ticket! As soon as a new shipment of fairy dust arrives we will be sprinkling you liberally. Your friends. The Orchard Fairies X

and the land girls pretended to be Uncle C and Bathgate puffing on their pipes and jawing, while the girls did all the work. We split our sides! The cake weren't half bad either! Simon said it was his best birthday ever.

Next morning I found this under my pillow ... see, I knew they'd come!

Sat 7th June 1941

COLONEL FLOSSIE!

Dear Diary, I been neglecting you again, but you must know by now that this is a busy time of year. The boys are helping in the garden or on the farm, while little Ellie and me is cooking to feed the starving! Tommy's taken to throwing a tantrum every time Frankie leaves him with me. Sometimes I feel like whacking him one – he just don't listen to me no more.

Still, I have some more good news from Auntie Ethel and Gramps!

I is a sergint, do as I says.

And I'm your flippin' colonel!

I wonders what Mum would do with him?

Monday 23rd June 1941
GERMANY INVADES THE SOVIET UNION!

Yesterday, and that makes it a SUNDAY, Germany invaded their friend and ally, the USSR!

Premier Stalin was caught on the hop, which isn't surprising, since it only seems like a few days ago that he and Hitler were top mates and sharing out Poland between them! The German panzer divisions are going to make short work of the Russians.

Mr Hitler is going to rule the flipping world.

Friday 8th August

Cook had a visit from the evacuee lady while we was at school: Maggie and Molly are to live with an aunt near London. We all feel really sad, but Cook says we don't have a say. They're to go tomorrow. Molly did me this picture.

flossy

my FRIEND

x x x x

Private, do not turn over.

Secret: I do want Simon to find his family – more than anything. But it would mean I might never see him again and he is like my best mate and my brother all rolled into one.

The news from the USSR is bad – the Germans are charging across the country capturing cities and thousands of them poor Russians.

Sat 9th August 1941 — A HORRID, HORRID DAY

Molly wouldn't let go of Cook. She put her little arms around Cook's neck and held on with all her might. In the end Cook had to pull her off and shove her into the car. We all cried and Cook kept worrying about them losing their "apple cheeks". I hope they'll write, but I doubt they will. I blames Mrs Mole. I hates her – she ain't got no heart. Now Simon has run off with Gracie. He ain't in the granary and Ellie is fretting for him. A BLACK LINE DAY

Later: Simon's back. He says he took Gracie for a walk on Merry Hill, but I reckon he's been crying. I expect a lot of Jewish kids held on to their mums, just like Molly held on to Cook, afore they was put on the train to England.

Tuesday 12th August

HAPPY BIRTHDAY!

We had a harvest tea for Tommy's birthday. Uncle Ron let him drive the tractor and ride on top of the hay bales! Best of all ... Dad sent him a card!

President Roo

President Roosevelt's picture was in Cook's paper. He's decided that US warships will guard American ships that carry goods to Britain. That almost makes them Britain's ally, that does.

October 25th — IT AIN'T GONE AWAY!

Dear Diary, I know it's been weeks, but I can't always be writing about the war. I like going enemy plane-spotting with Simon, Tommy and Gracie. Or shooting and trapping with Frankie – when he'll take me, which ain't often. Anyway, I got a letter from Miss Joan today, so here I am.

He'll be quite a dish if he ever flippin' grows up! →

I ain't taking no GIRL with me!

FRANKIE

MISS JOAN'S LETTER

Her car ain't rusted away yet, but it's covered in bindweed and moss!

Monday 3rd November 1941

Dear Diary, I fell asleep at school today! I told Miss Duncan I should be let off school now my family's so BIG. She said I could use the bed in her office whenever I wanted, but I was not to miss school.

Question: Will an education save me from the Germans?

Answer: Of course it flipping won't.

There'll be no leaving school ... think of your future!

If I have a future, I'll stay home and look after my dad.

Simon says I needs my learning because he don't want no daft idiot assisting him when he's a vet. He's the "daft idiot" – I'm going to be a nurse!

We found an icicle that was almost as tall as Tommy!

It is SO cold – we all got chilblains again, surprise, surprise. The Gramps Guard have stopped their patrols and started having meetings at the cottage. They march in wearing their great muddy boots and they've fair ruined our rug. I've hidden it now until the war's over, 'cos Mum made it and that makes it special.

That ain't mud, that's good cow dung, that is!

Frankie is our hero because he's taken over bog duty from Uncle C. Mind you, we ain't allowed to use it. We have to "Go at school, or not at all!"

Pooh!

Monday 8th December, 1941

The colonel came for assembly this morning and Miss Duncan asked him to tell us the news. He wrote it down for me because I'd be sure to get it wrong.

On Sunday December 7th 1941, the Japanese tried to take control of oil-rich territory in the Pacific. Without warning they attacked the US naval base at Pearl Harbour on the Hawaiian island of Oahu. Hundreds of Japanese planes dropped bombs on US battleships and aircraft, sinking or damaging eight US battleships and many planes. They then extended their attacks across the Pacific to the Gulf of Thailand, destroying more than 500 US and British aircraft. Without even declaring war they have managed to gain control of the skies and seas across the Pacific. Today Britain and the US declared war on Japan.

Why did Japan do such a terrible thing?

Japan was being so aggressive towards China that the US stopped trading with them, even in oil. So the Japanese, who need oil, decided to secure oil-producing areas in the Pacific for themselves, after first wiping out their most powerful adversary, the US.

THE NEW PACIFIC THEATRE

Does this make the US our ally!??

Yes! We are both at war with Japan, but the US is not at war with Germany or Italy.

Is Japan a very powerful enemy?

Yes, but they will live to regret attacking us without warning.

Miss D said prayers for everybody, even Emperor Hirohito of Japan. Sometimes I think you can just be too good.

AMERICA IS WITH US!!!!!!

Thurs 11th Dec 1941

GOOD!   BEST!   BESTEST!

Here is the news, brought
to you by Flossie Albright:

> Today, Italy and Germany declared war on the US!!!!! I shouldn't be
> pleased, but now the US will help us and we NEED help. We might even
> be able to win the war and rescue Simon's family. The war might end!

We is all very happy!

The land girls, the farm cats
and the fairies is happy too!

You is BONKERS, Mr Hitler,
if you thinks you can beat us!
We is about to FIGHT BACK!

U.S. DECLARES WAR ON THE AXIS

Friday 26th December   BOXING DAY

Dad came and went today. Oh, I miss him so – I can hardly bear his coming
no more, 'cos it just leads to his going. He was ever so chipper about the
Americans joining the war. He says that come the spring the Yanks will
be walking down the lane, whistling the tune of victory! I hopes so.
Dad brought us the Rainbow and the Beano for a Christmas treat.
I loves my dad and he loves his comics. He buys them for us and then
pinches them back "just for a quick read"!

I wish I could pinch him back "just for a quick hug"!

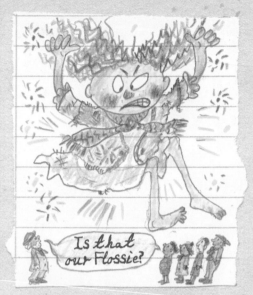

Is that our Flossie?

A NEW YEAR EXPLOSION!

Dear Diary, I said from the start that I'd give you the good and the bad, so I hopes you won't hate me for this bit of bad. I ain't making excuses, but I was choked Dad didn't turn up for Christmas or New Year. We was meant to go to Cook's tonight, for a "comfort meal", on account of the war dragging on and on ... but I never got there. I was at the door ready, when Serjint Tommy refuses to put on his coat and calls me his "horrid bossy sister". It stung me and I exploded worse than any flippin' bomb! I ain't proud of it, but that's how it took me. I yelled at everyone and then I yelled some more.

Uncle C sent the others over to Cook's, so I turned on you my poor diary and tried to rip and burn you. Well, Uncle C rescues you, and holds me on his lap and has a read of you, until I stop my blubbering. Then he fetches an old scrapbook from his chest, kept by my dad during the last war. All them years ago, he was writing about the Great War, just like I'm writing about this one. It made me feel so close to him that every inch of me ached and I started to snivel all over again.

KEEP OUT!

ARCHIE ALBRIGHT

SECRET

Then Uncle C tucked me into bed, called Gracie in to watch over me and went off to Cook's. I let Gracie into bed and we got stuck into Dad's scrapbook. It's much better than mine, 'cept my writing's neater and some of his stuck-in bits are yucky!

ARCHIE'S WAR
MY SCRAPBOOK OF
THE FIRST WORLD WAR
BY ME ARCHIE ALBRIGHT

TOE FLUFF

A BEETLE FROM THE BOG!

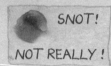

SNOT!
NOT REALLY!

Most of his is in comic strip; well it would be, wouldn't it?!
I might try some comic strip because now that I've seen Dad's...
I ain't going to burn you, my lovely diary and THAT'S A PROMISE!!

I ♥ my dad   He ♥ his dad

Dad's comic characters. →

— Wacko! Barko!

DUMPLING & GRAVY

It's late now and I needs some sleep,
else everyone will be up wanting breakfast.

PS The best thing about Dad's scrapbook is the happy
ending — the war was won and his dad came back to him.

Star light, star bright,
First star I've seen tonight.
I wish I may, I wish I might
Have this wish I wish tonight:

I WISH MY DIARY HAS
A HAPPY ENDING!

I'm going to have a rub of my lucky fairy acorn
and ask the fairies for the same wish.

2nd January 1942

This is my attempt at a comic strip — it's Fairy-me turning Tommy
into a pig, on account of him being so naughty! Only, I don't think
I got Dad's touch, so I'll stick to writing and doodling, if you don't mind.

You is a bossy, Flossie!

Naughty boys turn into pigs!

OINK!

Nobody mentioned the Flossie bomb … but Tommy wore his coat outdoors and in!

Sunday 1st February   A BAD NEWS DAY!

<u>In Asia and the Pacific</u> the Japanese are beating back the US and British.
<u>In Russia</u> it is freezing cold. The Russians are near starving and the
Germans have sent in more troops.
<u>In Libya</u> the British are still having problems with the Afrika Korps.
Simon drew me this picture of a
British Crusader tank fighting in
the Libyan desert.
<u>In the Atlantic</u> the Germans are
still torpedoing our merchant ships.

SAND!
SAND!
SAND!

Monday 9th February 1942

A red-letter day, as Dad used to say!

I got this brilliant letter from Miss Joan's friend in Egypt — I can't hardly believe she bothered with writing to me — it's the tops!

I wonder if I could ever be a VAD nurse?

This is the stamp. ←

I might have to do something about my hair!

NURSE ALBRIGHT

Tuesday 10th February 1942

You'll do, Flossie Albright.

Miss D is the best teacher.

I showed Miss Duncan my letter from Egypt and she read it out to the whole school! I asked if she thought I was clever enough to be a nurse for the Voluntary Aid Department. She said if I stopped saying "ain't" and "flipping", I could even be a Queen Alexandra Nurse and work for the army proper. ~~Ain't~~ Isn't that just the TOPS!

Nurse Flossie needs a bike.

Only how would I travel to Dorchester every day for training? And I ~~ain't~~ haven't ever taken an exam.

I took everyone for a run on Merry Hill after school to celebrate — they moaned something rotten about the cold — but it was GRAND!

What we walking in the dark for, Floss?

To thank them stars for our luck!

I feel happy!

88

Sunday 31st May 1942

The vicar was that gloomy today because last night 1000 RAF bombers bombed the German city of Cologne. If 1000 German bombers bombed London, Auntie Ethel would be sure to die. We prayed for the pilots and the German people.

After church Uncle Ron gave us our COGS Club badges, but I chucked mine. Our collections helped build them bombers. It's funny, 'cos neither Simon nor me saw any planes fly over here. I wonder where they all flew from.

I made a peace badge instead!

WORLD'S BIGGEST AIR RAID ON COLOGNE

Monday 1st June

ANOTHER BAD DAY

Simon found Pocket dead in the granary today. He says it was "due to natural causes", flipping vet! He made a little box and we buried it by Mum's sweetpeas. Simon said a Jewish blessing. He seems to know a few of these, but I don't like to ask too much about his life before us for fear he'll turn grey again. I know he loves us, but your own's your own. Besides, we do wrong things like eating bacon and that, but with rationing we're lucky to get bacon.

On the 1,001st day of the war more than 1,000 R.A.F. bombers on Saturday night flew over the Cologne area, and in 95 minutes dropped nearly 3,000 tons of bombs—the heaviest attack ever made in the history of aerial warfare.

The actual number of bombers engaged

Simon's Blessing
Blessed art thou, O Lord, our God, King of the universe, who has such as these in thy world.

For some it's luck, for others it's murder.

THIS IS SECRET!
DANGER...WILL EXPLODE ON OPENING!

Saturday 8th August 1942   WHAT A DAY!

Dear Diary, The summer holidays is flying by. We've been doing our war work, haymaking, gardening and food foraging. Uncle C says we'll do better in the autumn, but we've found:

Them's my babies!

mushrooms, strawberries, nettles, wild garlic and a few quail's eggs.

Only today I've had to find time to write these two BIG bits of news.

1. The Americans have had a GIANT victory in the Pacific! They have captured two of the Solomon Islands and driven the Japs into hiding on a third. Uncle C says this could swing the Pacific theatre our way!

2. FRANKIE HAS RUN OFF TO JOIN HIS DAD'S REGIMENT!
When I woke up this morning I found Ellie and Henrietta had gone, and this note under the covers:

> Dear Flossie, Don't be mad at me, girl, but I'm sixteen next week, so I'm off back to London to join Dad's regiment. I didn't tell you because I didn't want to set you off, or have Uncle C stopping me. I'm taking Ellie back to Mum — not because she ain't happy here, but I just think we needs to stick close. You are ever so special, Floss. If you weren't my cousin, you'd be my girl. See you after the war.
> Tell Simon I'll be on the lookout for his family.
> Ta-ta, Frankie x

DEEPLY SECRET:

I LOVE FRANKIE AND I LOVE SIMON – I LOVES THEM BOTH TO BITS!

Even my freckles blushed when I read it! I wish he hadn't gone, but Uncle Ron did just the same in the last war. I won't half miss him.

Simon is dead jealous of Frankie going, but he just isn't old enough to join up and no matter what he says, he'd never pass for sixteen.

It's flipping true!

Wednesday 12th August

HAPPY BIRTHDAY!

It's Tommy's 4th birthday today. Just fancy, he seems so old! Anyway, Cook gave him a special piece of birthday news. In fact I'm going to let him write it, because he is quite good at his letters ... if I hold his hand!

He's missing our Frankie!

20p is ratined ant I dnt ave to wash no mre! I liks dirt an ths is me dirty! Sgnt Tommy, esq. I's vry imprtant ant vry dirty!

Sunday 6th September   You have to laugh!

This afternoon we all went picking hazelnuts, even Cook. After a while it started to rain and I heard Cook swearing something terrible under her breath. I looked over and would you believe it – her stockings were running down her legs in brown streams! I nudged Tommy and Simon and we collapsed in a heap of giggles. Poor Cook. With clothes rationed, it's ever so hard to get stockings, unless you knit them – and they're a bit thick for Sunday best. So Cook painted some nylons on with gravy browning, seams and all! Oh my, oh my!

Tuesday 29th September   FOXY FOOD

Dear Diary, I need your sympathy. Uncle C shot a fox today. He says it was sniffing round the chickens, but I reckon he just wants to feed us some meat. He and Simon skinned and gutted it and Cook is going to show me how to cook it – I'm sure to be sick. Uncle C growled, "food's short, my girl, so you be grateful." Then he asked what we think the ham is, up at the King's Arms. "Pig," says I. "No, badger!" says he. Well, if that don't take the biscuit. Does that mean Simon could've been eating it?

I didn't see no fox.

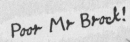

Poor Mr Brock!

91

Sat 3rd October 1942 — FOX STEW

purrfect

Prepare to vomit... poor Mr Fox has had a clean in the stream, so this morning Cook and me stewed him. I took the dish home and we had it for tea; Uncle C had forbidden me to tell the others what we was eating. I ate tatties. I checked the drawer later — not a morsel!

RECIPE
Cut the fox meat into handy bits, then brown in dripping. Add wild garlic and onions, cover with gravy and cook for one hour. Add root vegetables and cook for another hour. Serve piping hot with boiled tatties.

Weds 4th November
WACKO TO US!

I reckon them Gramps-Guard duties are getting to his chest.

Uncle C was ever so wheezy today, so he missed going to listen to the news. But it was so GOOD that Cook came rushing over. Since August, there's been this big battle going on around El Alamein in Egypt, and finally the BRITISH HAVE WON!!!!!

MEDITERRANEAN SEA

EL ALAMEIN

Western Desert

EGYPT

OUT

GET BACK DOWN YOUR RAT HOLE!

2 ain't enough!

The horrible Afrika Korps are retreating, dragging their rats' tails behind 'em!

10th December — A LITTLE EXPLOSION!

chilblains

Tommy's hand

chilblains

My foot

I had another of them explosions ... just a bit of one. It's so flipping cold and Tommy moans about his chilblains (and being hungry) morning, noon and night. There's next to no paraffin or candles and everyone is after kindling. We ain't heard if Dad'll be back for Christmas and Frankie ain't sent ONE letter. It's a bad, worser, worstest of days! Cook made marjoram ointment to sooth our chilblains, but I don't reckon she used enough marjoram!

11th December 1942   A BLACK FRIDAY!

Yesterday was not the worstest day – today is.
I loves Uncle C, except today
I HATE HIM!
I get back from school to find him about to drown a litter of kittens in a bucket. He said there weren't enough food to spare. I yelled something shocking and kicked over the bucket – then Simon grabbed the kittens and we scarpered. We've hidden the kittens in the granary, but it's that cold, I don't think they'll live. Simon says we'll have to feed them with Tommy's old bottle.

WARNING
BUCKETS
CAN BE
DANGEROUS

In the hands of a mad adult!

They've still got their eyes closed.

Star bright, star light,
First star I seen tonight,
I wish, I wish, this wish tonight:
That the kittens live, that Uncle C and I is friends again and that Dad and Frankie keep SAFE.

I'll rub my acorn and make a fairy wish too.

PING!

That Flossie is getting a touch demanding!

Saturday 12th December 1942

Dear Firebrand Flossie.
We sprinkled your Uncle C with fairy dust and hopes he'll come to his senses!
Love from your fairy friends
PS Them's magic petals. Any more trouble, put one in his tea!

When I wake up this morning, I found this note pinned to my pillow addressed to "Firebrand Flossie"!
I peeped out from the curtains around my bed and saw an old box beside the fire holding a mother cat and four fluffy kittens!

HE'S A FLIPPING COUGH DROP,
my Uncle C. How does he think I'm going to feed all them extra mouths?!

93

I did not eat badger ham and I did not let Sjnt Tommy or Simon eat it neither!

Sunday 14th February 1943

We ain't had a treat for yonks, but today Uncle C took us to the King's Arms for lunch. I think it was on account of Valentine's Day and him and Bathgate being sweet on the Land Girls - only he said it was to celebrate the Russians having chased the Germans out of Stalingrad, which is very good news. Watch out, Mr Hitler, then Russians is going to chase you all the way back to Berlin!

Love's not just for the young'ns.

UNCLE C SAYS

Tuesday 23rd February
IT'S RAINING LETTERS!

We had ever such a quiet start to the year, with no word from anyone, but now we've had a flurry of letters! One was from Auntie Ethel, to tell us that Frankie did join the Middlesex Regiment and has gone for training up north.

I copied this from Dad's book!

Auntie Ethel can't go back into the Fire Service, on account of her arm not bending proper, so she's going to train as a nurse with St John Ambulance!

St John's badge
Soon I'll be able to leave school and train as a nurse too.

Ellie did Simon this picture; I think she misses him!

We also had...
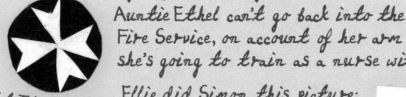
A COMIC CARD FROM DAD!

What a flipping miracle... follow the mouse and there it is!

START

OOPS!

Hey presto!

What ho, my lovelies!

Hitler permitting, I've wangled a weekend pass for the start of March. Keep your eyes peeled for an oldie wobbling down the lane!

Cheerio and chin-chin,
Dad. X

Flossie Albright
Honeysuckle Cottage
High Barn Estate
Nr Dorchester
Dorset

OH ... I just can't wait! You won't believe this, Diary, but I got _two_ more letters for you! I reckon the postie's been nesting on them!

I AM KEEPING THE BEST UNTIL LAST... AS IS MY WAY!   NEXT a newsletter and a _uniform button_ from Petty Officer Mole!

POOR MISS JOAN, SHE MUST HAVE BLUSHED FOR BRITAIN!

AND NOW... DEAR DIARY, COMES THE BEST... A LETTER FROM FRANKIE!

Just to let you know I'm still around and thinking of you all! Tell Simon not to let Uncle C carry anything heavy, his gammy leg's worse than he lets on — and tell that Tommy to be good, or I'll box his ears!
Chin up girl, Frankie X

THIS IS HIM ON THE DAY HE JOINED UP! DON'T HE LOOK LIKE A FLIPPING FILM STAR! Tommy being good is a laugh. He now refuses to answer all questions because "Mr Hitler be a-listening!"

Sat 6th March 1943 MY FAVOURITE OLDIE COMES HOME!

I woke up this morning to find Dad and Tommy jumping on my bed – daft beggars! Uncle C was cooking Dad's favourite breakfast of fried tatties and egg. We didn't tell him he was eating the only egg because he'd shot a wild duck for our tea. Shame it set Tommy off on his favourite duck rhyme!

We took the duck up to the big house and had our tea with Cook, the land girls and Mrs Rose, who was over from Dorchester.

Oh, it was tops to be with my very best dad! Tommy was good and all!

It was a pintail duck.

I was gooder and gooder.

What shall we have for dinner Mrs Bond?
It's goose in the larder and duck on the pond.
Ducky, ducky, ducky, ducky come to be killed.
Ducky, ducky, ducky, ducky come to be killed.
You naughty little ducklings, I feed you every day,
But when I want to kill you, you all swim away!

He doesn't seem to mind Mr Hitler "a-listening" to his singing!

Sunday 7th March   TO THE SEASIDE

My bestest, bestest dad let us off church today and took us to the seaside!!!! We nearly didn't go, on account of Uncle C not being up to the walk, only Dad weren't having it. He bundled Uncle C into Tommy's old cart, along with a blanket, a flask of tea and a loaf of bread, and we all helped to push!

KEEP OUT!

Most of the beaches around here have been mined, to keep the Germans from landing, but Dad's fisherman friend, Mickey, had told Dad where to go. It was scary at first, with all them soldiers in gun turrets and barbed wire everywhere, but after a bit we got used to it.

MICKEY!

As we walked down onto the beach,
Mickey was bringing in his catch, so we
all set about collecting driftwood and built
a fire fit to cook a fish feast! I thought the
smoke might attract a German submarine, but
the soldiers didn't seem worried. We boiled crab in
seawater and wrapped dab and mackerel in seaweed
and cooked them over the coals. I reckon we fed
a whole regiment of soldiers and fishermen,
but we still had a wacko blow-out!

The soldiers told us that the army uses the area
for testing bombs, rockets and floating piers, which
scared me even more 'cos we only live over the hill. They
laughed and said over Weymouth way the kids build their
sandcastles in the shadow of warships and submarines!

We played beach cricket, built pebble castles and skimmed
stones until the evening light fell and we could see the
German guns firing from across the channel. On the
way home, Dad gave Uncle C a piggyback ride and
Simon and me pushed Tommy in the cart.
We was pooped, but we all agreed it was
the best of days. I collected all these
treasures to remind me of the day.
I found a special shell to put on
Mum's grave – she loved the sea.

My record for skimming stones is three jumps!

Mon 8th March 1943 A SAD, GLAD DAY

When I woke Dad was gone, but he had left me a note!

Dear Flossie,

Sorry love, I did kiss you goodbye, but I didn't have the heart to wake you. I won't be back for your birthday so I've left you Mum's old camera; you'll be able to use it to take pictures for your diary... I also found this photo of her on the beach a few years back.

Your mam would be that proud of you, Floss, you're the tops. Don't let that ruffian brother of yours upset you and tell him and Simon, ta-ta and wacko from me, Dad x x

PS Don't forget to harvest as much free food as you can and send anything you can't eat to Ethel. You can also earn a few bob collecting nettles for making into vitamin pills.
I know ... I sound just like the old codger!

Ain't I the luckiest? I got me mum's camera and a lovely picture of her!

A decision: I ain't going to be a nurse, I'm going to look after my dad and our Tommy — Mum would like that.

Dottie Rose Sky

Monday 5th April

Simon is looking after 3 orphan lambs ... the kittens are right put out!

NURSES FOREVER

KEEP THIS FLAG FLYING!

The whole world needs nurses, Flossie Albright!

Cuckoo!
Cuckoo!
Cuckoo!

Sunday 11th April

Spring has sprung!

Primroses

We heard our first cuckoo on the way to church and I put primroses on Mum's grave.

Thurs 29th April 1943

I am writing this very, very small, 'cos I don't want Simon to ever, ever see it. There are terrible, terrible rumours about the Nazis killing thousands of Jews in Poland. I won't never let them take Simon. I've hidden a hayfork under my bed, just in case.

Friday 14th May 1943

Flossie's war news has been a bit quiet lately, but

YESTERDAY, THE ENEMY TROOPS IN NORTH AFRICA SURRENDERED!!!!!!

I wonder if Miss Joan's friend, Nurse Gregson, will come home now?

Monday 17th May

I am writing this in code. (The key to it is hidden somewhere in this diary ... beside a red dot! Well, I might forget it one day!)

Mvdh uiln Klozmw hgroo gviiryov - klli, klli, kvlkov. R zn hl hxzivw lu
gfhg zylfg vevibgsrmt nld - gsv mvdh tluh uiln tllw gl uorkkrmt
gviiryov rm hvxlmwh!

Tuesday 18th May

Here is the news with Flossie Albright: The RAF has damaged some German dams with a new "bouncing bomb" invented by a Mr Barnes Wallis. They bounce along the surface of the water, just like our skimming stones! They could even have been tested on that very same beach. The idea was to stop German munitions factories having electric power, but a damaged dam causes flooding, and flooding kills innocent people and animals...

A DAM-BUSTING RAID!

SUCCESS AT FOURTH ATTEMPT

The full official account of the raid on the dams in South-West Germany was given by the Air Ministry last night in the following statement:

For many weeks picked Lancaster crews had been training for one operation. They worked in secrecy on a bomber station which, as far as possible, was cut off from any contact with the outside world.

Only about half a dozen other men in the whole of Bomber Command knew what they were doing.

21st May SIMON'S BIRTHDAY!

Gracie brought Simon a dead rat as a special treat. You can always count on her when it comes to presents!

I hate war. Uncle C says it's a great victory and I'm starting to sound like a bleedin' pacifist, same as our Ethel.

Weds 2nd June   SAD NEWS

Mrs Mole has just told me something ever so sad. After the Axis troops surrendered in North Africa, Miss Joan's friend decided to return to England. She was travelling in a convoy of six ships and two of them were torpedoed, one was hers. Poor Nurse Gregson is missing, presumed drowned. I feel ever so sad.

25th June MY BEST EFFORTS!

I've been trying to take some photos with Mum's camera, so I'm leaving space here for my very first and best efforts!

Miss D

The Colonel

Saturday 3rd July

Dear Diary, Wait 'til you read what Miss Joan has just sent me ... you won't believe it!

I can't believe this has been sent to me! Of course I'll flipping treasure it!!

BRITISH F
SOCIET
6, MIDA
CA

OHS

Use this envelop

W.R.N.S
Speckington Manor

Dear Flossie,
          Just a quick note ... we are so busy here.
I know that Mother told you the sad news of Julia Gregson's death. What you won't know is that she was awarded the Africa Star for her nursing in North Africa. As she had no children, her husband would like you to keep it safe in your diary. He says that she often thought of you writing away in yours, as she wrote in hers!
     This is a great honour, so I hope you will treasure it.
                    Petty Officer Mole

Sat 21st August

We went whortleberry picking today! They're used to dye uniforms blue, so we get a whole 1/- a pound for 'em! We're blue from top to toe, but bluest of all is the tongue of Sjnt Tommy, followed by Gracie's. Dogs and young'ns seem to prefer eating to picking! Well, worts is yummy! Some pilots think worts help them see in the dark, so me and Simon are going to save our sugar ration and make wort jam to sell up at Warmwell.

Cook's "wort" comb

Wednesday 8th September 1943 — THE ITALIANS SURRENDER!

The colonel was going to take us rambling this afternoon, but instead he made us garden while he told us the GOOD NEWS: Last month Italy's fascist dictator, Mussolini, was forced to resign and Marshal Badoglio formed a new government without one fascist in it. Now Italy has surrendered to the Allies!

Gardening gives me backache.

Marshal Badoglio

13th Sept — TOP NEWS... THE YANKS ARE HERE!!!!

I haven't seen them yet, but Miss D told us that American Army engineers are here setting up camps for the combat troops! Miss D thinks that there'll be an Allied invasion of Europe soon. Ain't that ripping? I hugged Simon when she told us – now we can find his family!

Sunday 26th Sept — NO YANKS SPIED YET!

Auntie Beth says she had some Yanks in her shop ... but we haven't seen even a distant glimpse of one. I'm fit to burst.

Sunday 3rd October — IT'S TRUE – THEY'RE HERE!!!!!

Dear Diary, I flipping saw them! Well, at least two of 'em, driving past the church in a jeep. They was ever so friendly – we all cheered and they waved!!!

Hiya, kids!

Beep!

Italian soldier – now our friend!

Wednesday 13th October — IT'S A MAD, MAD WAR!

I'm writing this upside down as the whole world is topsy-turvy, so I might as well join in: Italy has just declared war on Germany! Miss D says they've "come to their senses", but I don't get all this changing sides.

101

Thursday 14th October 1943   FLOSSIE ALBRIGHT - WAR HEROINE!!!

Would you flipping believe it - I captured a German!!!
We were on our way to school when we passes this man
that looks like a scarecrow. I turns to have another look
and spot fur-lined boots beneath very short trousers.
It didn't add up, but I acted very cool until we rounded
the bend, then I dashed like the devil to Uncle Ron's.

OUR MODEST FLOSSIE

Oh no,
it was
nothing

DESERVES A MEDAL

He thought I'd gone soft in the head, but later he comes
to tell Miss D that she has a heroine in the school -
the man was a German pilot! His plane had crash-landed
during the night, so he'd changed clothes with a
scarecrow. But as a scarecrow has no feet, yours truly
spotted his disguise! He's been arrested and taken to
a prisoner of war camp. Uncle Ron says I deserve a medal.
When I think how close Simon came to a German I turn
cold all over. Mind, he didn't look dangerous, just scared. He might be
made to help on Uncle Ron's farm.

WHAT AN ADVENTURE - I CAN'T WAIT TO TELL DAD!

Sunday 17th October 1943

The Gramps Guard held a ceremony
for me at the King's Arms today.
They said I was "a fine example of a citizen
defending her country from invaders!"
The whole pub applauded. I felt that
chuffed and was bought more fizzy pop than
me, Tommy and Simon could burp down!
(No medal - worse luck.)

FRIEND OR FOE?
BE SURE YOU KNOW!

KEEP ALERT
(like our Flossie)

Thurs 25th November   YANKS RAIN CHOCOLATE!

Lorry loads of Yanks drove past the school at playtime and
when we waved they threw us chocolate bars! There was ever
such a scramble, but Tommy got one ... of course.

HE WON'T SHARE, THE LITTLE BLIGHTER!

Later: I found a squashed bit of chocolate on my pillow! This is
the paper it was wrapped in ... genuine silver, from a US chocolate bar!

26th November 1943

Came back from school to find Uncle C and Gracie both poorly. We put Uncle C in the camp bed by the fire and Bathgate fetched the doctor, though I don't know how we're to pay for him. Simon braved Uncle C's grumps and brought Gracie inside.

The doctor said Uncle C should be in hospital, but he won't go. So we have to give him special medicine three times a day. I WISH I WERE A PROPER NURSE!

HE CAN'T BLOOMIN' DIE!

← Cook's pee jar!

Cook brought over some soup and a pee bottle!

Saturday 27th Nov — TWO CHEERY LETTERS!

I read 'em both to Uncle C, but he's not listening, no more is Gracie. I've put her on Uncle C's bed.

I LOVE MY COUSIN FRANKIE!
Sssssh, don't tell!

Dear All,
        Just to let you know about your grand relations! Gramps and me were in a parade and marched past Mr Winston Churchill! He looked grand – if anyone can sort out this war, it'll be him. I'm working full-time for St John's Ambulance now and really feel I'm helping without hurting. Gramps is still our ARP star, which isn't bad for 68, but I miss Bernie – he hasn't had any leave for a while now. I enclose a note from Frankie and "Night Bombing" by Ellie.
                Love Ethel
        Thanks for the food parcel.

FLIPPING SHOW-OFFS!

Hello m'hearties, Here I am in Camp Oswestry. We ain't doing much, just kit inspections, rifle range, map reading, the odd beer with the lads. We're all a bit browned off, but hope to get a spot of home leave soon.

Chin-up, Frankie

PS can you forward this picture to Tommy. Cheers. X

Watcha mate, This is my backpack, it's even heavier to carry than you!
    In it I try to fit:
Water bottle, mess-tin, knife, fork, spoon, pullover, stove, groundsheet, jack-knife, mug, fuel blocks, face veil, blanco, wash things, towel and some sweets!

Friday 17th December 1943 — DAD'S HOME – WORSE LUCK!

Uncle C's been really poorly, so I ain't had time to write. I give him his medicine, but he don't perk up. Gracie ain't good, neither.

Now Dad's come home to move Uncle C into a nursing home, Simon into the big house and me and Tommy to Auntie Beth's.

WELL, WE WON'T GO! We ain't managed all this time just to be split up now. I may not care for Uncle C that perfect, but I done it better than a flippin' stranger would. Besides, if him and Gracie is split, one of 'em is sure to peg it.

Dad says he ain't arguing, as he has to report back tomorrow, so we're all to be ready first thing. Well, we ain't flipping doing it!

A smudge from an angry tear. THIS IS AN ANGRY LINE!!!

Sat 18th December 1943 — THE SIEGE!

We've locked ourselves in the granary! Dad is banging on the door and swearing words that don't come out of no comic.

Bloomin' kids!

DAD

This ain't like you, Flossie.

COOK

I ain't waitin' all day.

BATHGATE

Have I time for a nap?

TRIXIE

SAY WHAT YOU LIKE, WE AIN'T BUDGING!

We promised Simon he'd stay with us and I WON'T break that promise.

Mrs Rose
Our Saviour
1943

LATER: Phew! Dad was about to break down the door when it all went quiet. We listened through the cracks and heard Mrs Rose, who was over visiting Cook, offer to take some time off work to nurse Uncle C. Wacko! We can stay together after all.

Secret: I'm glad to have help looking after Uncle C ... I don't want him to die.

Now I am drawing a line under this!

Sunday 19th   HOORAY, NO CHURCH TODAY!

The fog was that thick, Mrs Rose and her nipper could hardly find their way over from the big house (where they're staying) so we didn't go to church. Instead, Mrs Rose cooked us eggy-bread! She made Uncle C eat a bit and gave him a wash – she was ever so kind.

None of us could get Gracie to go out, not even Simon.

I unravelled an old sweater and started to knit Frankie some gloves – I'll never get the hang of them fingers. Simon wrote and asked the Red Cross to find his family. Tommy made a camp under the table. We's short on logs.

Mon 20th December

Too foggy for school, but guess who braved it to visit us? Miss D. Me, Tommy and Simon are to be in our "best" by eleven tomorrow, for a special surprise. I'm going to wear my blue ribbon.

Tuesday 21st December 1943

A DAY TO
REMEMBER
! ! !

Eleven o'clock prompt, a Yank in a jeep appeared out of the fog. He was that smart in his uniform, I thought of Frankie! He called me "ma'am" and opened the jeep door with a salute – we was struck dumb! We whizzed all the way to Dorchester. Our Tommy was steering half the time, so it's a miracle we got there! We pulls up in front of the big hall, the driver jumps out, opens the door and says, "Folks, your party awaits."

I can't stop blubbing.

Thursday 23rd December

A GREAT SADNESS

I couldn't write yesterday – I was too sad. Our Gracie has died. She just went to sleep and didn't wake up. Me, Tommy and Simon wrapped her in a sack and put her in a box full of straw. We cried a lot and each put a present in. I put in a slice of bread and dripping, Simon his lucky rabbit's tail and Tommy a promise..."to be kind to dogs and never, ever biff 'em"! Him and his promises.

The ground was too hard to dig, so we built a mound of stones over the box. We decorated it with notes, asking the fairies to keep our Gracie safe until the spring, when we'll bury her proper.

We each drew our happiest memory of Gracie – so she won't ever be FORGOT! Simon and Uncle C have taken it bad.

Tommy →

She ate my fatty bits and never told.

← ME

She knew when I needed a cuddle.

Simon

Every day she made it special.

Saturday 25th December 1943

CHRISTMAS DAY!!

A BAD CHRISTMAS FOR PIGS AND CHICKENS!

Our dad came home... YES HE DID!
Uncle C got out of bed...
YES HE DID! We had a REAL chicken, not a furry one... YES WE DID!

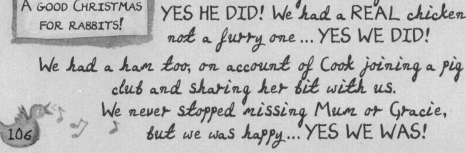
A GOOD CHRISTMAS FOR RABBITS!

We had a ham too, on account of Cook joining a pig club and sharing her bit with us.
We never stopped missing Mum or Gracie, but we was happy... YES WE WAS!

I think we've all got more hope now that the Yanks are here!

Andy arrived loaded down with gifts, tins of fruit, butter, sugar, Coca Cola, chocolate and some REAL silk stockings for Cook and Mrs Rose... they was blushing for Britain! No more gravy browning for them! Dad says the local girls pay no attention to British Tommies now the Yanks are here with their bloomin' silk stockings!

Uncle C managed to play his accordion for a bit, and we all sang and danced – it was like old times. I ate a whole tinned peach and danced with Simon, Tommy, Dad and Andy!

IT WAS HEAVENLY!

What's more, Diary, I'll be fourteen years old next year and able to leave school. I think I'll wear scarlet lipstick and marry a Yank!

HAPPY CHRISTMAS

Them's really my lips!

LOVELY DIARY!!

I AIN'T GOING TO WRITE NO MORE, ON ACCOUNT OF WANTING TO END

✻ 1943 ✻

ON THIS HAPPY NOTE...

AND YOU NEVER KNOWS WHAT TOMORROW MIGHT BRING.

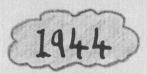

1944

THIS HAS GOT TO BE
THE LAST YEAR OF THE WAR!

SCRUMMY CHOCOLATE

Monday 14th February 1944   Got any gum, chum?!

We got a new game at school that's better than skipping! We hang over the playground wall waiting for Yanks to throw us chocolate and chewing gum.

IT DRIVES MISS DUNCAN WILD!

I've never seen gum before – the chew goes on forever, but not the flavour!

Things is that different now the Yanks are here. It's like we're not living in the country no more.

On Sundays the church and the pub are full of Yanks, which is lucky 'cos Uncle C isn't up to the walk now and he can always get a lift. I don't know where they get the petrol from, but them Yanks don't seem to have heard of shortages!

NO ... I ain't mentioning St Valentine's Day, 'cos I'm going to keep my love secret ... even from you, you nosey old diary!

HAPPY

BIRTHDAY!

Tuesday 21st March
MY 14TH BIRTHDAY!

Dear Diary, Meet the new Flossie Albright, all grown up and old enough to leave school! Only now, Lord flipping Beveridge has changed the school leaving age to fifteen! Miss Duncan says they're not sticking to it while the war's on, but in my case she's insisting.

SO I HAD TO GO TO SCHOOL TODAY - STINKING!

Trixie's shoes

My shoes

Sssh... I got starter boobies.

SECRET

Bathgate took us in the trap as a very slow treat, Trixie being as old as the hills, but it were better to wear out her shoes than mine! Cook gave me a birthday tea in her kitchen and we was just cutting the cake, when Mrs Mole burst in, yelling at Cook for entertaining in _her_ kitchen. She said she'd enough riff-raff in the house, without giving tea to the odd-job man's daughter. I wanted to run home, but Cook said to ignore "the stuck-up old moo", as she's just fed-up with the war and missing the general.

A STUCK-UP OLD MOO

The Red Cross still ain't found Simon's parents. I'll be the unhappiest happy person in all the world when they do.

<u>Weds 22nd</u> Two US officers have been billeted in the big house, and it weren't only Mrs Mole who exploded this time. You could hear Cook's "Oh mys" across the yard! Anyway, they both turned sweet on hearing that the officers would bring their own supplies. Guess who their driver is? Andy! Oh my, oh my!

Yes, Ma'am

ANDY

Wacko, Birthday Girl! You's practically grown now... sorry I didn't make your birthday, but you might see an oldie wobbling down the lane soon!
X X X X
Dad x

Don't wait up for me, I'll be late!

MY FLOSSIE - ALL GROWN!

<u>Thurs 23rd March 1944</u>

A BIRTHDAY CARD FROM DAD ...LATE!

Yup, I feels it!

Me too!

Friday 24th March 1944   SOMETHING IS A-STIRRING!

Uncle Ron says it's not only Dad who's due home soon –
Auntie Ethel is expecting Uncle Bernie and Frankie.
Soldiers often get leave just before a battle and Cook
says she feels in her bones "something is a-stirring!"

Tuesday 28th March   LAST DAY OF TERM!

We finished school early today and went to see if Uncle Ron
had any orphan lambs – he hadn't. Simon was that miffed,
Uncle Ron asked him to stay over and lend a hand!
I weren't pleased, on account of doing his chores, but
then Andy tooted and offered Tommy and me a lift, so I was all smiles!

He gave me some <u>war news:</u>
<u>The Japanese</u> are still causing the Allies problems and they've
even tried to invade India. But they <u>won't be</u> invading
Britain, because the Allies will sort them out in the Pacific.

Remember

Hitler has big ears!!

I'm writing this next bit in code,
'cos Andy says it is <u>TOP SECRET!</u>
Tvmvizo Vrhvmsldvi, gsv Bzmph hfkivnv
xlnnzmwvi, rh zylfg gl erhrg gsvm!

Now don't that mean something is afoot? When I asked
Andy he just winked and flashed his snowdrops! He gave
me this photo of Eisenhower, or "Ike" as he calls him. →

Wednesday 29th   I HATE BOYS – I DO, I DOOO!

Tommy and me went to fetch Simon home, but
he's staying over until lambing stops. It takes the
flipping biscuit – he's meant to be MY friend.
   He says Uncle Ron's dog is having pups –
hint, hint. Well, he ain't having one, 'cos he
won't be here forever and I'm not talking to
him NO MORE. Tommy wanted to stay over too;
I had to drag him home.

NOTICE

This person is no longer Flossie Albright's friend.

YUCK

Sunday 9th April — THE BEST BESTEST EASTER DAY

Dear Diary, It's grand — everyone's home: Dad, Miss Joan and the general. We all went to church, even Uncle C, and the vicar read "The Tolling Bell" by John Donne, which did us in.

No man is an island, entire of itself; every man is a piece of the continent, a part of the main; if a clod be washed away by the sea, Europe is the less, as well as if a promontory were, as well as if a manor of thy friends or of thine own were; any man's death diminishes me, because I am involved in mankind, and therefore never send to know for whom the bell tolls; it tolls for thee.

After, Dad took us on a surprise picnic in Teal Meadow. We paddled in the stream, played cricket, read comics and made daisy chains. Andy joined us later with a load of treats and bunches of "daffo-dilles" for me and Cook — I think the land girls were jealous. Simon came home with us afterwards — not that I flipping care!

I dedicate this happy day to Mum and Gracie.

We missed Maggie and Molly.

A blusher: I've never been given flowers before!

A fairy wish: Please let this good time go on for EVER. Flossie ✕

If I ain't too old for wishes.

Monday 17th April 1944

Dear Diary, We've had such a fine week, with everyone home! I'd almost forgotten how things used to be. Poor Simon, I bet he hasn't.

Dad helped:

Uncle C — GET THE GARDEN STRAIGHT

Flossie — GET THE HOUSE STRAIGHT

Tommy — GET HIS MANNERS STRAIGHT

AND SAID SIMON CAN... train him a pup, ready for when he gets out of the army — which means we'll be getting a "widdler" SOON! I don't know what the cats will think.

SAY NO TO A PUP.

111

Tuesday 18th April 1944 — A BLACK TUESDAY

Everybody left today. I feel an ache and my eyes is pricking. I'm ever so scared that something BIG is about to happen, and my dad might not come home again ... not ever.

BLACK

We heard your wish, young Flossie, but times always change, good and bad. Your Fairies xxx

Tuesday 25th April — WARNING – THIS IS A RESTRICTED AREA!

HALT!

We are surrounded by tank traps and road blocks, and have to get permission to go anywhere. We're not allowed to travel by train or have visitors. Simon and me snuck up Merry Hill to see if the Germans were landing, but all we saw were ships flying barrage balloons!

LATER: I waited for Andy in the lane. He said I should stop fretting because the war news is brilliant: The Soviets are fighting back through Poland and Romania to Germany, and the British Allied forces and the US are pushing North through Italy. Then he winked and told me that if we could push a few Allies through France to the West – THE WAR WOULD BE WON!

YANK SPEAK

Sweet = candy   Lorry = truck   Petrol = gas   Pavement = sidewalk

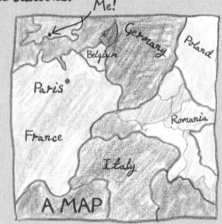

Me!
Germany
Belgium
Poland
Paris
France
Romania
Italy
A MAP

Weds 26th April — A SCARY LAST DAY OF THE HOLS!

Simon went lambing AGAIN! So I took Tommy out to see what was going on. We'd just made it up Merry Hill, when a soldier stopped us. He said we was entering a forbidden area and had best go home – my knees shook! I showed him our identity cards, but he wouldn't let us through.

I reckon Simon'll turn into a lamb one of these days!

THEN we heard a sudden rushing of wind and a huge barrage balloon went flying over our heads! It must have broken its anchor ropes. It got lower and lower and finally there was a loud explosion and a rush of flames ... right by Uncle Ron's farm. Poor Tommy, I hardly let his little legs touch the ground for fear Simon or Uncle Ron were caught in the fire. We arrived to find the balloon still smouldering, along with a hayrick, but luckily nobody was hurt.

Simon says we must stay close together, and Uncle C wants one of the land girls to walk us to school each day. Mrs Mole won't like that!

Friday 5th May 1944   A BLUSHER AND A HALF!

I've not read this letter to anyone.
I've always thought a lot of Miss Joan, but she must be flipping DAFT to write me a letter like this – ain't I already got Tommy to care for?

THIS IS VERY, VERY PRIVATE.
FLIPPING CHEEK!

21st May SIMON'S BIRTHDAY
He hoped the pups would be born, but they weren't!

Sunday 28th May   WOOF...WIGGLE ...WOOF!

After church Auntie Beth had us over for dinner, because ... the puppies have been born and WE got to choose ONE!!!!!!

Dinner with our Beth, that's a bloomin' first!

Hope you ain't hungry! ↓

No girl pup could ever match our Gracie, so we've decided on a dog. He's the cheekiest little squiggler and we've named him Young Georgie, after Old Georgie – the dog that Dad had during the last war.

YOUNG GEORGIE

Curls

Pink nose   Eyes still closed

We can't bring him home until he's eight weeks old, but Uncle Ron says we can visit every day, if his mum don't mind. She says, "woof, but you got to bring me a treat!"

Cour-se I flipping will!

Our Gracie R.I.P.

It seemed the right day to bury our Gracie. We dug a big hole for her and filled it with wild flowers and kisses.

A STORM IS BREWING!   <u>Saturday 3rd June 1944</u>

Uncle Ron started haymaking today, and we went to help. Not really – we went to see Young Georgie! His eyes are open and he's just such a "Schnuckel, Schnueffelein", as Simon says. ♡ ♡ ♡

We left early on account of all the army vehicles about, the extra tents going up and the flocks of planes flying over. Cook says there's nothing on the news, but all the activity is making us jumpy. What's more, we haven't seen Andy or his officers for TWO DAYS.

It's so hot!

<u>Sunday 4th June</u> A BUSY NIGHT

There was a giant storm last night and we saw hundreds of bombers lit up by the lightning. Uncle C made us run through the rain and wake everyone in the big house, then we all scrambled into the cellar. We was dripping wet, so Cook braved Mrs M's scowls and gave us blankets and hot cocoa. WE WAS SCARED! Uncle C tried to cheer us with a ghost song, but Cook said his "ooking ghosts" were worse than a ton of flipping bombs!

Ooooh, aaaah!

Tommy snuggled on Cook's knee and asked her to be his mum; she laughed and said she was too old. I hope Dad don't marry again. I don't want a new mum. There were no bombs, so we went home for breakfast.

Quick march!

<u>Mon 5th June</u>   STILL NO NEWS!

We had a Gramps Guard escort to school today, but it was too hot to work. There are still planes flying over and troop trucks on the road. My stomach is churning and nobody seems to know what's going on. Uncle C wouldn't let us visit Young Georgie after school; he said we was to stay close to home.

114

Later: It's almost midnight and I'm sitting under Gracie's apple tree, writing by the light of the moon. It's too hot to sleep and the noise of planes is constant. I can see them as clear as day, all flying towards France. Some of them is towing gliders.

Tuesday 6th June 1944   Almost sunrise

The planes woke Simon too, so we climbed Merry Hill. We expected to be stopped, but there were no soldiers; just loads of ships! They moved across the water towards France like silent monsters. We're INVADING EUROPE! Isn't it grand? Oh I do hope we can rescue EVERYONE. Simon and me <u>held hands</u> and wished for that on the last star afore dawn.

I didn't know it before, but there's holding hands ...and holding hands!

    We saw Cook on the way home. She said to get ready for school and then come back with Uncle C to listen to the 8 o'clock news.

Here is the BBC news, as told by Flossie Albright:

We have reliable information that the combined forces of the British Commonwealth, the US and patriots from occupied Europe left the British coast in the early hours of the morning for France.

MY DAD IS THE BEST!

We all cheered with relief – something is happening at last! Then I remembered Dad. Uncle C says not to be daft, he'll be at his usual lookout post, but I don't know. I wanted to stay with Cook and listen to the next news, but Uncle C weren't having it.

I thought school would never end. Lilly came to fetch us home and we made her run all the way, which was just as well, or we'd have missed listening to the King's speech up at the big house. Speedy Simon wrote some of it down for me: →

Four years ago, our Nation and Empire stood alone against an overwhelming enemy, with our backs to the wall. Tested as never before in our history, in God's providence we survived the test... After nearly five years of toil and suffering, we must renew that crusading impulse on which we entered the war and met its darkest hour... At this historic moment surely not one of us is too busy, too young, or too old to play a part in a nation-wide, a world-wide, vigil of prayer as the great crusade sets forth.

After the anthem, Mrs Mole actually suggested tea in the kitchen. She hasn't heard from the general, and the US officers left without a word. Poor soul – for all her money, she looks worn.

A posh cuppa!

NOW THAT THE INVASION HAS COME THE WAR WILL SOON BE OVER!

Thurs 8th June NEWS FROM DAD – BUT NO NEWS FROM FRANCE

We've all been a bit jumpy today and then to cap it all, we had a card from Dad.

KEEP MY DAD SAFE!

Then comics have made him soft in the head – what's "wacko" about going off to fight the Hun?

Friday 9th June Mr Postie delivers again!

Everyone is calling the invasion the D-Day landing, and I think this letter must have been written just as they were setting off.

It is from... FRANKIE!

Dear Floss, Dad and I are in a truck heading south. We don't know where we're going, but all leave has been cancelled, so it must be something big. I hope so; I can't wait to send the Hun packing! Only open the enclosed letter if the worst happens. Otherwise, I'll be expecting it back – unopened.

Your best cousin, Frankie   PS Salute Simon and the nipper for me.

I ain't ———→ saying more than that, 'cos I don't want to think on it.

I hid the other letter under my mattress; then I wrote a wish note to the fairies. On Sunday I'll ask the vicar to pray for my family, special-like. God might listen more to a vicar than the likes of me.

<u>No news from across the Channel.</u>

← Can't wait to have YG home!

Tues 20th June   A NEW GERMAN BOMB!

I been so caught up in the D-Day landing that I ain't given a thought to London, but today the postie told us about a new German flying bomb; he called it a "Doodlebug". It has an engine and streaks across the sky until the fuel runs out. Then it crashes down, leaving no time for the people below to take shelter. You're safe so long as you can hear it, but if it cuts out ... BOOM! You're about to be blown to bits! I'm that worried about Auntie Ethel, Ellie and Gramps.

I'M COMING, READY OR NOT!

<u>Wednesday 21st June</u>   STILL NO REAL NEWS!

Cook says 125,000 troops landed in France on that first night, and more were dropped inland. The Germans have got guns all along the coast, so hundreds of soldiers must have been shot. I WON'T BLUB, but I do want my dad home ... please, please let my dad come home.

I'm sending my wish up to the highest star.

<u>Thursday 22nd June 1944</u>

Me and Uncle C both had a letter today. I'm sticking them in, 'cos they are both important.

Cook's going to write to Maggie and Molly's auntie, to ask if they can come back here away from them Doodlebugs.

Dear Flossie.
Thanks for your last wish-letter.

Here is a four-leaf clover. It's almost as powerful as fairy dust, so keep it safe and it should help. X

Ain't they kind!

<u>22nd</u>, <u>23rd</u>, <u>24th</u>, <u>25th</u>, <u>26th</u>, <u>27th</u>, <u>28th</u>, <u>29th</u>, <u>30th</u> <u>June 1944</u>

NO NEWS OF DAD, NO NEWS, NO NEWS, NOT A FLIPPING WORD!

SPOT THE
DIFFERENCE

A BISCUIT

ELLIE →

<u>Sat 1st July</u>   WE GOT ONE HOME SAFE!

We was about to have tea, when Uncle Ron turns up with our
Ellie. The poor little 'un, her face was grubby with tears.
Gramps decided he had to remain "on duty" in London, so he'd
put her on the train in care of the guard. She sat on my knee
and hugged me so tight I thought I'd pop! Simon conjured a
biscuit from behind her ear and Tommy promised not to pull
her pigtails for a whole week – you got to be cheered by that!

ANSWER: There ain't none, 'cos Ellie's face is as round as a biscuit!

<u>Wednesday 5th July</u>

I had a letter from Frankie today – I ain't taken it all in yet.

Churchill – British

SOME
OF
THE
TANKS

Panzer – German

M4 Sherman – US

Tiger – German

There ain't much to say after a letter like that. Poor Frankie – he's
only a kid, really. I'm ever so glad I made those pull-throughs.

<u>Thursday 20th July</u>   THE SCHOOL HOLIDAYS START TODAY!!

Miss D's going up to London to work for St John's Ambulance, on account of
the Doodlebug casualties. They're aimed at London, but they're fired from as
far as Holland, so there's no telling where they might land... I won't
think on it. I wish I could go to Dorchester and do a First Aid Course.

Sunday 23rd July

The sky is full of planes again – it's just like the Battle of Britain days! Sometimes we see a dogfight, and yesterday I saw a plane go down in the Channel.

That's the third today.

If we see a British pilot do a victory roll, we all cheer, 'cos we know he's had a hit. The Germans are trying to bomb the supply ships and the ships bringing the wounded back from France. Bathgate says the roads around Dorchester are packed with lorries and ambulances. He went to The Keep for news of Dad and the General, but there weren't none.

Secret: I don't think it does a jot of good going to church, but what if I don't go? Will God take his anger out on Dad? I wish Mum was here to tell me things – Uncle C just shrugs ... but I loves him anyway. ♥!

Monday 24th July 1944   THE WIDDLING WIGGLER!

I'm letting Simon write this, on account of it being his special day!

I'm so proud to write in the "Great War Diary". Well, the news are WE'VE GOT YOUNG GEORGIE!!! He's inside my shirt right now, snoring his little nose off! I'm going to make him the best and most obedient dog in the World. I will report regular about his progress. I believe he doesn't miss his mum because he's got me! He's a real "schnuckelchen" as we say at home.

His first curl!

Our Floss and Simon is tryin to take my best new puppy from me. Uncle C says we got to share him, but I wnt, hes mine and I'm going to call him Lassie and tech him to put them chkns to bd, so's I dnt have to do it no mor. Tommy xx

We have to pretend YG is Tommy's pup, or he goes wild. We had to help him write his bit ... but don't tell him I said that!

I love our Tommy and Young Georgie!

119

Tuesday 25th July

We had a note from Gramps today and Uncle C's been digging ever since. He won't talk and he won't eat. I didn't really know Uncle Bernie, but I feel sick for Ellie... we ain't told her yet.

Dear Col,
   We had a telegram to say that Bernie was Killed during the Normandy landing. We don't have no details, but Ethel has taken it bad. I think you will have to tell Ellie, because I don't think her mum's fit to travel.
   Pray for young Frankie,
                    Arthur.

Wednesday 26th

Kids!

Uncle C told Ellie about her dad and she just said, "Can he see me if I'm a naughty girl?" Poor mite - I think her dad's been away for so long, she don't really understand. Later, she did this picture of her dad. I'm ever so sad, sad, sad.

Sunday 30th July 1944   Simon's Puppy News

NO NEWS OF DAD!

Good = His nose is almost quite black. He follows when I call him. He'll sit ... for half a second.
Bad = He chewed Trixie's harness and Bathgate almost strangled him.

Tommy's Puppy News

Growl!

Lassie is vry good. He eats my scraps so Floss dnt find em in the drwer no mor. Tommy x

I likes birthdays!

Saturday 12th August 1944

HAPPY SIXTH BIRTHDAY, OUR TOMMY!

> If it ain't bombs, it's flying flowers!

We had a grand day picnicking and making corn stoops for Uncle Ron. Cook made a cake, with real eggs instead of powdered, and Tommy gave _his_ "Lassie" the first piece! Mrs Rose brought over a shirt made out of an old skirt. Tommy loves it; he looks like a field of wild flowers. She'd made Ellie a little rag doll with the scraps, which was right kind.

He thumped me when I said that! → It don't seem a day since Tommy were in nappies and sucking on his bottle.

Sat 26th August

PARIS IS FREED FROM THE HUN!

We heard yesterday that the Allies have liberated Paris - ain't that great! We celebrated by picking strawberries and raspberries. I can't say where, 'cos there's always spies about and we don't want no one else finding them. They're just so flipping good with cream and a sprinkle of precious sugar!

Wild ones is sweeter than garden grown!

This Morning's War News
France
Paris liberated by Patriots after four days' fighting; Allies thrust far into France; pincers closing. (P1)
Allied army enters Marseilles: Americans' 150-mile thrust takes Grenoble. (Pp 1 & 6)
Nazis fired field guns at Paris Patriots. (Pp 1 & 6)
"Little Paris" in London celebrates; singing in streets. (P6)
Mr. Eden pays tribute to France. (P3)
Nazis face disaster in the West; battle of France near climax. (P6)
Cherbourg in use ahead of schedule. (P3).

Simon's Puppy News
Good: Young Georgie learnt today to pick raspberries.
Bad: He ate them, rather than putting them in the basket.

Tommy's Puppy News
My Lassie made a hole in my soc.
Floss said she'd clip my er if I dnt stop him.
He ws havin fun so we ran awy and ate strwbs.
We was both sick, they ws good.
I loves him and all my family.

Friday 1st September

A note from Dad,
A NOTE FROM DAD,
A NOTE and PHOTO
FROM DAD!!!!

I AM FIT TO BUST!

Sorry, my spiffo family – you must be worrying, but sending news is tricky. I'm pretty chipper. We're doing well and hope the end is just around one of the next bends. I pray it is. Keep safe, Dad.
PS – a photo of bath time for you!

Sunday 10th September 1944

A NEW GERMAN BOMB – THE V2

The vicar told us that a new bomb, the V2, fell on London yesterday. It's bigger than a Doodlebug and travels at the speed of sound, so you don't hear it <u>arrive</u> until <u>after</u> it's exploded! Poor Auntie Ethel and Gramps. It makes you wonder who'd invent such evil.

Monday 11th September   EXCITING WAR NEWS!

<u>The Allies have reached Germany!</u> The Hun are fighting back something fearsome, but there'll be no stopping us now!!!!

12th September   MORE EXCITING WAR NEWS!

The "blackout" has been changed to a "dim-out". And ... Bathgate and Uncle C have been stood-down from defence duties. They're not pleased, but I am – IT MEANS WE AIN'T GOING TO BE INVADED and Uncle C don't have to hang about in the damp – bless his tin hat!

Sunday 17th September   "MAKE FOR THE DITCH!"

We thought a V2 had exploded when we was crossing the fields, but it were Halifax bombers towing gliders towards France. I hope they're carrying more troops and supplies to help my dad.

I asked them to carry my love with them to DAD x

Monday 18th September 1944

Just don't think on fear!

More planes today. EVEN Uncle C thinks something's afoot.

Sun 1st October A TERRIBLE BLACK DAY!

The vicar told us the Allies have failed to capture a bridge at Arnhem in the Netherlands. Loads of soldiers were killed, including some from the Dorsets. I couldn't breathe no more when he said that, let alone pray for the brave men who died trying to rescue their mates from the River Rhine. I ran outside, thinking my only dad might be dead.

I told Uncle C that I was going to The Keep for news, and he sent Simon with me. I wished Andy were around to give us a lift; it took an age to get there. Then, when the desk sergeant said Dad _had_ been at Arnhem, my legs just buckled ... but he _weren't_ on the casualty list!

I burst into tears and I'm crying now at the thought of it, 'cos I loves my dad that much. They was ever so kind and gave us a cuppa and some biscuits, and a couple of soldiers gave us a lift home on the back of their bikes. Young Georgie loved it! What a wobbler – as Dad might say. I wish I had a bike!

TROOPS FERRIED ACROSS RHINE BY NIGHT

Thurs 12th October   A VERY GRUBBY NOTE FROM DAD!

Hello my lovelies, Here I am in the muddy ▓▓▓▓▓ we've been getting into a few scrapes, but I'm OK. I miss you something terrible and don't ever want to go away again.
  Keep your chins up, Dad x

The censor must have blanked that word out, but I reckon it's "Netherlands".

We don't never want you to go away again, neither.

123

Me holding my breath! →

Friday 1st December

It seems as if we is all holding our breath, waiting for the war to end ... except for Ellie, Tommy and YG who just play all day.

Simon's Puppy News

YG is a little cracker! It seems as if he doesn't mind to sleep out in the cold. We fetch him indoors when nobody sees it, but Uncle C's a bit cranky some days, because of the rheumatism in his gammy leg and his wheezes. I'll teach YG to be a sniffer, so he can find lost people and things. A little schnüffelhund!

Tommy's Puppy News

My Lassie is the bestest puppy in the hole wrld and galxy. He knws he blngs to me and not poo-poo Simon. Me and Eli is frnds now and If she slips on the ice lassie helps her up. I'm going to tel my dad he's a wako puppy.

So who do I belong to?

Mon 25th December   A BLACK CHRISTMAS

I'm in the granary with Simon and he's making me write this down because it's news, but I can't stop crying.

My lovely, lovely cousin Frankie has been shot by a sniper and is dead. He's dead and I won't ever see him no more and little Ellie won't stop her crying – he was that good to her.

Please, please don't let my dad be killed too, oh please not. I don't know what to say no more, it's all so terrible and I want my mum so bad.

Tuesday 26th December

Miss Duncan walked through the snow to say how sorry she was. Ain't that just like her. I showed her Frankie's unopened letter and she sat with me while I read it ...

I decorated
these pages
with my wild
flower collection.
Each of them
flowers is filled
with love
for you, Frankie.

I'm going to bed now.
I hurt too much for sitting,
I need to be curled.

Thurs 28th December 1944

When I woke up Miss Duncan was sitting by my bed, with
Ellie on her lap. The reason for her being there came
to me with a terrible ache, but I thought of Frankie's
letter and got up with a smile. I'd been asleep for two
whole nights and a day. Miss D made us breakfast, but
Ellie crawled under the table. Uncle C called Young Georgie
in to join her and we fed them both with bits off our plates.

After breakfast Uncle C sent us over to help Cook because
Auntie Ethel and Gramps are arriving later and Auntie Ethel's
going to share Cook's room.

Later: They arrived, but Auntie Ethel don't talk; she just
rocks herself like a baby. Her hair has gone grey; Gramps said it
just happened overnight. She don't seem to see any of us,
not even poor Ellie.

I'll be strong for you, Frankie, but not if my Dad dies.

Six months later:

Frankie was awarded this medal for bravery. Auntie Ethel
let me take a rubbing of it. She sleeps with it under her pillow.

1945 STILL AT WAR!

Monday 1st January 1945

While we've all been sorrowing, there's been a terrible battle in the Forest of Ardennes, Belgium. There was thick fog and snow, which gave the Germans the chance to force back our allied line.

> All news from the Ardennes front yesterday was of Allied gains and German losses. Echternach was recaptured by Gen. Patton's American Third Army, while on the northern flank other forces thrust south-east to captured Manhay and Grandmesnil.

They nearly had us beat, then the weather cleared and we bombed the blighters – now we're pushing into Germany again.

Tuesday 9th January   WOULD YOU BELIEVE IT!

ME! HEAD GIRL

Dear Diary, It's my last term at school and Miss D has made me HEAD GIRL ... I got a badge to prove it!

HEAD GIRL! Mum would be that proud. When I told Auntie Ethel, she didn't smile, but she touched my cheek.

Cook hugged the breath out of me and made a special tea! Mrs Mole came in, but she didn't tell Cook off. She shook my hand and gave me a whole tanner! She says the general is certain to bring Dad home safe. Oh, I wish we was all celebrating together: me, Mum, Dad and Frankie.

Cook made fairy cakes!

Weds 10th January   I GOT A LOVELY FAMILY – I HAVE SO!

When I woke this morning, Young Georgie was licking my face and Simon ... yes ... Simon, was cooking "celebration" head girl porridge!

Simon's porridge – LUMPY!

We took Auntie Ethel to school, 'cos Miss D has asked her to help with the little ones. Miss D thinks of everything – she does!

I wore my badge!

Wednesday 31st January 1945 CAMP AUSCHWITZ

It's no use keeping this news from Simon because everyone's talking about it. Soviet troops have found a German camp near Auschwitz, in Poland, with over two thousand starving Jewish prisoners. The Soviets think thousands more Jews were murdered before they arrived. Simon has gone off with Young Georgie — Uncle C says to leave him to come back when he's ready.

This here is a line of love for all them poor people and their families.

Thursday 1st February

I took some warming bread and milk out to the granary first thing, and there was Simon. We didn't talk, but he ate it all and then we set off for school. Auntie Ethel put her arm around Simon and Ellie held his hand. There's nothing to say, 'cos none of us know where his family might be and false hope don't help.
Even Tommy was quiet.

YG was waiting outside school for us, just like Gracie!

Thursday 15th February 1945 WE BOMB DRESDEN

Hello, freckles!

In assembly Miss Duncan told us that the RAF have been bombing the German city of Dresden for two whole nights. She said it was on account of them making weapons there, but it were a grand city and many civilians will have died. The colonel coughed and said it would bring an end to the war. We all prayed he were right.

I saw a snowdrop out — it made me think of Andy. I hope he's still alive ... somewhere.

(I ain't writing no more on this page — it don't seem respectful.)

Dresden, the great German railway, road and industrial centre was the main target for the heavy bombers. During Tuesday night it was twice blasted by R.A.F. Lancasters. Yesterday the American Eighth Air Force struck the city again.

The R.A.F. dropped nearly 650,000 incendiaries, many 8,000lb and hundreds of 4,000lb high-exposive bombs. Flames could be seen 200 miles away.

Thurs 1st March   WAR OR NO WAR – SPRING STILL SPRINGS!

Here is the News, brought to you by our very own Flossie Albright.
The Soviets are gaining ground in eastern Germany,
while our Allied troops are close to the west.
We have the HUN on the RUN!

The sun shone clear this morning and everything is in bud.

Sticky-bud

Wednesday 7th March   US TROOPS ENTER GERMANY!!!

GREAT NEWS! US troops have crossed a bridge over the Rhine
and into Germany! I bet Andy led the way in his jeep!

Sunday 11th March 1945   Up AnD dOwN wE gO!

The vicar told us the US have been dropping incendiary
bombs on Tokyo, in Japan. The fires have killed so many
people; he thinks they'll surrender soon.
We prayed for the Japanese, the Allies, the
Germans, the wounded, the dead and the
grieving – the whole flipping lot.
I put a kiss on Mum's grave – she's best out of it.

I love
you,
Mum

Sat 17th March 1945
Our Young Schnüffelhund!

Flossie doesn't let me write much about Young Georgie,
because her diary has not many pages left and the
war has not ended. But I must tell you ... he's
already the best tracker in the whole county!
This is him a few weeks ago taken with Flossie's camera.

I got to tel you that Lassie is
lovin only Elli and me, so ther!

This ere is m thum
print that provs it.

Thurs 29th March   MY LAST EVER, EVER, EVER DAY OF SCHOOL!

I can hardly believe Simon and me will never go back to school again. As head girl I had to give a talk in assembly. I was that nervous. Simon and Uncle C helped me write it...

This war started in 1939 and now it's 1945, and we all hopes the end is close. During this time I've grown from a little girl into a "head girl", and I am ever so proud to have been head girl in our own village school. All through this war Miss Duncan and the colonel have made it a place of safety, where all are welcome: local kiddies, evacuees, the much too young and the much too old! We've been one big overgrown family; we've dug together, learned, sung, played and laughed together. And we done it all in peace, no matter what... and that's something grand.

My Uncle C says we've shown true English grit, and he should know, 'cos he bakes that in our bread every flippin' week! So I says, three cheers for Miss Duncan, who showed us the way and helped us through, and three cheers for all them old boys, including my cousin, Frankie, who were brave and fought for us!

I'm pinning my badge in here, so's I don't never lose it.

Everyone cheered, and then Miss D presented all the leavers with a poetry book. I blubbed, blushed and grinned! I won't half miss school.

Wednesday 18th April '45
BERLIN SURROUNDED!

We all thought the fighting would be over by Easter, but no such luck. Tommy's gone back to school now, so I don't even have him to distract me. Anyway, today we heard that Allied troops have surrounded Berlin, our Simon's home town, but I'm not counting my lambs!

Am I too late for Easter?

Yes!

Fri 20th April 1945 — STILL NOT COUNTING!

Uncle Ron's got more lambs than I can count,
but no news of peace ... yet.

Sat 21st April — KAMIKAZE PILOTS

We helped Uncle C in the garden today and he told us that some
Japanese pilots, called "kamikazes", are loading their planes with
explosives and then crashing them into Allied warships, near Japan.
That's brave that is – and very, very terrible. Uncle C says the ships
have no defence against them.

Sunday 29th April — STILL NO CHURCH BELLS!

We felt sure the vicar would tell us that peace had
been declared, but he just rambled on about patience.
We all felt very flat.

Tommy says he hates my "ration cooking".
Well I can't flipping help it.

> I ain't eatin' green yuck, no more!

Weds 2nd May 1945

THE DEATH OF HITLER WAS ANNOUNCED OVER THE GERMAN RADIO SHORTLY BEFORE 10.30 LAST NIGHT. IT SAID THAT IT TOOK PLACE AT HIS COMMAND POST IN BERLIN, NOW ALMOST COMPLETELY OCCUPIED BY RUSSIAN TROOPS.

This is the Soviet troops on top of the German Parliament

BLIMEY!

Dear Diary, You WON'T
believe this ...
Mr Hitler has
killed himself.
Have you ever heard
the like? I ain't. I was in and out of Cook's kitchen
all day, hoping peace would be declared, but NO.

Uncle C and Bathgate say that peace is fine and
dandy, but they don't want to lose "their lovelies".

BATHGATE

LILLY

Remember,
Diary, them's
the land
girls they'd
hardly
speak to at
the start!

UNCLE C

JOLLY

130

MISSING

REWARD 1/-

OUR SIMON

Wednesday 9th May 1945

Maybe we're just a bit tired today, but we've all felt down. The war won't really be over until Dad's back, safe and sound, and who knows when that'll be. What's more - Simon's gone missing. He weren't there when we woke this morning and he's not in the granary, or anywhere else, as I can see.

LATER: We searched everywhere for Simon and then Sjnt Tommy had a bright idea: get Young Georgie to track him down! We gave him a sniff of Simon's stinking socks and off he shot, across the fields to the school. He sniffed around a few times, but there was no sign of Simon.

THE FINEST NOSE IN THE COUNTY.

It was getting dark, so I was just about to grab YG and go home, when he ran off towards Miss Duncan's cottage. We peered inside and there was Simon!

Poor thing. I should've thought - now the war is over he's desperate to find his family. Miss D says she will contact the Red Cross again, and a Jewish group that helps to reunite families.

Then she said the moment had come to get her motorbike and last can of petrol out of mothballs! So we set off home, with a ROAR!

I think Dad is going to be ever so chuffed with such a well-trained dog!

When we got home Cook cheered us up with some tasty food left over from yesterday and we looked through the newspaper at pictures of the VE Day celebrations. The war news keeps getting better 'cos today Germany surrendered to the Red Army in Czechoslavakia.
It must be all over soon!

Thursday 7th June 1945 — A LETTER FROM ANDY!!!!!!

How happy am I? HUGELY happy... no HUGELY, HUGELY happy!

Dear Flossie,

Here I am on a troop ship, sailing back to the US. I can't say I'm sorry, but I'll miss you all at High Barn, especially my young freckles!

You were the first Brit to invite me into your home. So I've written to Jim, at the smithy, and if you wander up there in a couple of days, you may find he has a little something by way of a "thank you" for making a Yank feel so welcome.

Say hi to everyone and tell Cook that I was only teasing - her apple pie really is as good as my mom's.

Your good friend, Andy xxxx

I'll always treasure his letter. Simon and me is going to collect the little'ns from school tomorrow and go on to the smithy - I can't wait to see what it is ... maybe it's a lucky horseshoe.

Friday 8th June — TING-A-FLIPPING-LING!

Dear Diary, That smithy... first he said he hadn't heard from Andy and then he said he'd _lost_ whatever it was. I nearly cried! Then he laughed and sent us out front with our eyes shut. All of a sudden, we heard a ting-a-ling and there it was - MY BICYCLE!

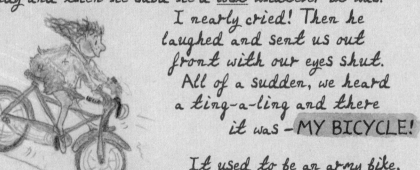

It used to be an army bike, but Andy's had it adjusted for me. It's got lights, brakes, a reflector and a BELL ... oh wacko!

We all had a go on the way home and I fell off EIGHT times! Simon says it's a good way to scrape off some freckles ... the cheek! Oh, lucky me.

Secret: Now I can learn nursing in Dorchester without having to leave home! I think I'll be a midwife and travel about on my bike, bringing babies into the world and caring for their mums.

133

Oscar, Delta, Oscar... I'm home!

Saturday 9th June 1945 — MISS JOAN RETURNS

Miss Joan came home last night, so this morning I waited for her in the stables. I showed her my diary, not to read like, just so she could see I kept it up. She was dead impressed and said she'd let me into a little secret...

Dsvn svi uirvmw Kvgvi tvgh srh wrhxszitv, gsvb'iv tlrmt gl tvg nziirvw! gszg'h tizmw, gszg rh.

She thinks our dads'll be home any day now. I DO HOPE SO.

Me Tommy
Ellie

I let Simon have a go with my camera.

This is Simon in his Sunday best.

Me not wobbling on my bike!

I practised on my bike for the rest of the day. Tommy, Simon and Ellie are SO jealous!

Monday 11th
NOT A MOUSE TO BE SEEN!

Remember me?

I'm sitting in the granary, with Young Georgie pushing at my hand for a stroke. I been looking for a mouse, but I can't find one. I'm all out of sorts; I miss my friends at school and Miss Duncan. Simon goes up to help Uncle Ron most days, but Uncle C says I got to talk to Dad first if I want to start nursing. Trouble is, I don't know when he'll be back. We had a scribble from him today, but "soon" could mean any flipping time!

See you soon, my lovelies. Spiffo, Dad.

The Japanese kamikaze pilots are still crashing into US warships. Over 300 have been sunk or damaged. They'll have to run out of pilots one day.

Tuesday 12th June 1945   FLOSSIE, THE EXPERT CYCLIST!

I cycled to Dorchester today. I only fell off twice and that weren't my fault! I went and looked at the hospital and The Keep, but I didn't dare go inside either of 'em. There's going to be a General Election soon, and there were posters everywhere, which is daft, 'cos we all know Mr Churchill's Conservative Party will win – he's our hero!

Bumps in the road or tank traps!

Saturday 16th June

"Hoy, don't splash my posh diary!"

We decided to cheer ourselves up by playing hooky. We ignored our jobs, packed some sandwiches and escaped to Teal Brook. Simon and Young Georgie are giving Tommy and Ellie swimming lessons – more like splashing lessons if you ask me!

FLIPPING KIDS!

SECRET: Dear Diary, I thought on VE day everything would magically return to how it was before the war, but it isn't like that. Things seem even worse: Auntie Beth has hardly a morsel to sell in the shop, and Cook has started slicing eggs with a razor blade. That way she can make one egg do four sandwiches – you got to be desperate to do that. Simon still has NO news of his family and to top it all we've never heard a word from Maggie and Molly – and Cook is that hurt.

ENOUGH OF THIS, it's time I showed them how to swim the Flossie way!

Will they have lost their apple cheeks?

Thursday 5th July   VOTE CHURCHILL, IT'S ELECTION DAY!

Uncle C says it's rude to ask people who they voted for, but I don't need to. You'd have to be flipping nuts not to vote for the man who helped us win the war!

Tuesday 10th WONDERFUL, WONDERFUL NEWS!

The Red Cross has sent Simon a letter from his _mum_!!!

He tore off to school with Tommy and Ellie to show it to Miss Duncan.   I AM SO HAPPY FOR HIM.

The letter is in German, but Simon has translated it for me:

PTO ➔

135

My Dearest Simon, To hear from you at last – it is a miracle! Your sister and I are safe and well, but the Red Cross has told us that your papa was sent to Auschwitz and they have no news of him after that. Mally and I have escaped over the French-Swiss border hidden in a hay wagon – we were very, very lucky. Since then, we are in a refugee camp in Switzerland.

I promise to you that we will be together again as soon as I can find a way. I have at the moment no money and nothing left to sell – but we will be together again, my darling, brave boy.

Thank the family who are caring for you, and ask them please, to let you stay a little longer.

You must be almost a man now and I am sure you can help them a great deal. I wonder if you will recognize your mama when you see her again?

My love to you, Mama

Wednesday 11th July 1945   A DIFFERENT SCARED

MY MUM AND MALLY BEFORE THE WAR

By Simon

I found Simon crying in the granary last night. He made me cry and all. It's hard to know, but I think he's scared for his dad and scared he won't recognize his mum. You'd think he'd just be happy to have found his mum and sister, but they've nothing, not even the fare to England. Sometimes knowing is trickier than not knowing.

I am writing this in code, because not even I know how I feel.

Mum would've told me:

Hrnln'h yvvm nb yvhg nzgv zoo gsilfts gsrh uorkkrnt dzi, zmw R wlm'g dzmg srn gl ovzev. Zmw R wlm'g dzmg srn gl szgv nv ru nb wzw xlnvh slnv zmw srh wlvhm'g. Sld hslfow R uvvo? Dszg'h irtsg gl uvvo? R wlm'g uorkkrnt pnld.

This grey

Thursday 12th July 1945

Simon has gone all grey and silent. I think he went and asked Uncle Ron's gaffer for a farm job, but he ain't saying.

We hear ya!

Fri 13th "Oh my, oh my, we must try!"

I went to ask Cook if we could help Simon's mum and she took me to see Mrs Mole. I was dead scared, but Miss Joan was there and I had to speak up for Simon. Mrs Mole asked if he was trustworthy - Cook said he was top notch and magic with animals, bless her. Maybe Friday 13th weren't the best day to ask, but we'll wait and see.

Saturday 14th

MRS MOLE TO THE RESCUE!

I prescribe freedom, not the pot.

Simon the vet!

Mrs Mole has asked Simon to help Bathgate with the horses ... FOR REAL MONEY! She'll give Simon a bit and send the rest to his mum through the Red Cross. The land girls are leaving soon and there's no news of the old stable lad, so Simon is to take his place!

Mrs Mole has also offered to sponsor Simon's mum, if she will come and work in the big house - just until she gets sorted. Uncle C says if he had the room, Simon's mum would be his guest, not a flipping servant. But Mrs Mole means well, and Simon's mum needs a job and a sponsor to come to England. Simon is to stay with us for as long as he needs to, then he'll quit the stables and go to veterinary college!

Thurs 26th July   WE'VE GOT A NEW PRIME MINISTER

It's Mr Clement Atlee. I feel a bit sorry for Mr Churchill though after all he did for us in the Battle of Britain.

Sunday 29th July   DING DONG!

It's so good to hear the church bell calling us across the fields. I prayed really hard for Dad and Simon's family, while the vicar prayed for the soldiers in the Far East. It's so far away; I has to keep reminding myself the war's still going on there. Last month the US captured the island of Okinawa, and their airforce keeps bombing the cities ... but the Japanese still ain't surrendered.

JAPAN — Pacific Ocean — Sea of Japan — Tokyo — Hiroshima — Okinawa

Mon 30th July A CERTAIN PROMISE!

All that whistling - I can't hear myself tweet!

Simon ain't stopped whistling since he became the stable lad ... but I ain't sure it's a happy whistle. Waiting to hear from his mum is flipping agony! So I'm promising, here and now, not to write no more until:

A. We hear from Simon's mum.
B. The war with Japan ends.
C. We have news of Simon's dad.
D. We have news of my dad!

WHISTLING

STINKING OF MUCK!

HALF CLEANED TACK!

Tues 7th August 1945   US DROPS AN ATOMIC BOMB

Smoke hides city 16 hours after greatest secret weapon strikes

THE BOMB THAT HAS CHANGED THE WORLD

I can't keep that promise - the news is that bad. Yesterday, a US plane dropped a thing called an atomic bomb on the Japanese city of Hiroshima, a supply depot for the Japanese army. President Truman says the bomb is 2,000 times more powerful than any other bomb and it will help to end the war. There ain't no news of casualties on account of a huge cloud of dust over the area.

I'm only a flipping dove, what can I do?

Wednesday 8th August   BLACK NEWS

The Japanese radio is saying that "enormous devastation" has been done to Hiroshima and thousands of people killed ... just from one bomb. They still haven't surrendered. Now the Soviet Union has declared war on Japan too - it don't look like this war'll ever end.

I'm drawing these lines under today, 'cos it's all got to stop soon.

Thurs 9th August 1945
ANOTHER ATOMIC BOMB

The bomb was dropped by parachute.

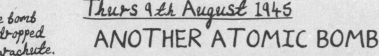

The US have dropped another of them atomic bombs on the port of Nagasaki. Smoke rose to over 50,000ft. Now they're dropping leaflets warning the Japanese people that they'll drop more and more bombs until they surrender. I pray their emperor won't let no more people be killed.

WHERE IS MY DAD?
I needs him home; things is so black.

This is what the bomb looks like when it explodes.

Tuesday 14th August   COOK'S NEWS!
Cook called us in to listen to the 6 o'clock news, so we knew something was up.

JAPAN HAS FINALLY SURRENDERED!

As our new prime minister,
← Mr Clement Atlee, was pleased to tell us:
"The last of our enemies is laid low ... for the moment let us all relax and enjoy ourselves in the knowledge of work well done."

He's soft in the head! How can we enjoy ourselves? Don't he know about all the people that's wounded, bereaved, homeless and hungry? Plus this terrible new bomb that's going to be around for ever and ever. It don't bear thinking about you stupid flipping prime minister.
Tomorrow is a public holiday and we are all supposed to celebrate Victory in Japan Day,
BUT WE AIN'T IN THE MOOD.

I could wear this rosette and sing and dance, but I flipping WON'T!

Weds 15th August 1945

Do you agree?

Oh my, I think I do!

All the people in London thought VJ Day was worth celebrating.

Oh my, they're agreeing!

For once Cook and Mrs Mole have agreed on something! There'll be no celebrating at High Barn until the general and my dad are home safe. So we just did our chores, had a comfort tea with Cook and listened to the King's speech.

Ellie and Sjnt Tommy were "sick of speechifying" so they went and ate the last of Uncle's C's raspberries – likely he'll skin 'em alive! Tommy is real good to little Ellie. Maybe I ain't done so bad by him – though I say it myself as shouldn't!

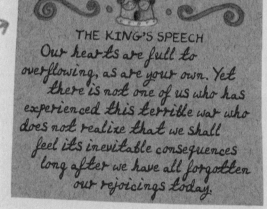

THE KING'S SPEECH

Our hearts are full to overflowing, as are your own. Yet there is not one of us who has experienced this terrible war who does not realize that we shall feel its inevitable consequences long after we have all forgotten our rejoicings today.

Thurs 16th EVEN AUNTIE ETHEL IS SMILING! SIMON'S MUM IS COMING TO HIGH BARN!!!

We're all so happy. It might take months to happen, but that don't matter, 'cos now we know it will!

There's a sad bit though: Simon's mum also wrote that, although they shouldn't give up hope, the Red Cross thought that his dad had died in Auschwitz. Simon, being Simon, don't want to talk about it. He says he'll think on that when his mum and sister are safe with us.

But I can't stop thinking on it now.

Fri 17th August '45   FLOWERS FOR ALL!

I got up ever so early and made a picnic breakfast.
Then I woke Tommy, little Ellie and Simon and led
them to the top of Barrow Hill, 'cos that's where
Dad went at the end of the Great War. We sat and
watched the sun rise up and turn the sea red, while
we dunked Uncle C's gritty bread into sweet milk.

Then we picked armfuls of wild flowers and threw them
high into the air, while we thought of all the poor
people killed and injured in the war. We thought of
Uncle Bernie, Frankie and Simon's dad. We wished Simon's
mum and sister a safe journey here, and our dad and the
general a safe return. And somehow we all felt that
much better. We had a big hug and a few tears
and then we rolled all the way down the hill,
bump, bump, bump, with Young Georgie barking alongside us!

I got the bruises to prove it!

Saturday 18th August 1945

Simon was up with the lark this morning, mucking-out the stables.
He stank when he came in for breakfast, but he's
chipper, so we all feel better. I helped Uncle C
in the veg garden; the sun shone and it was
fine. We picked a huge bunch of sweet peas, so's
to make the whole cottage smell sweet. Then
Cook, Auntie Ethel and the young'ns jumped out
at us, carrying lemonade and a birthday cake.

Boo!

With so much going on last week we'd all forgotten our
Tommy's birthday! He promises faithful to forget mine next year!

This is the last page of my diary and Dad's not home — what to do?

141

<u>Sunday 19th August 1945</u>   IT FLIPPING WAS!!!!!

Oh Diary, You'll never guess who was bouncing on my bed when
I woke up this morning? It was our Tommy with

... our ... very ... own ... DAD!

Yes it was, yes it was, yes it flipping was!

He nearly squashed me flat, the daft beggar.

Can you see the
fairy dust, Floss?

I didn't let
him in, honest!

HERE ENDS MY SECRET WORLD WAR II DIARY
ON THIS, THE 19th AUGUST 1945,
THE WAR HAS FINALLY ENDED
FOR ME, FLOSSIE ALBRIGHT.

PS I might write another diary about living in peace and becoming a
nurse, or I might flipping not! One thing's certain though, I
got to thank you, my dearest Diary. I'd never have got through
these last six years without you. You've been ever so patient, you never
once told me off and best of all — you've kept my secrets safe.

PPS This here is a picture of Mum's
best rug - it's out again!

• A ~ ♥ ~ H •